FOC AND FANCY TEA

Baker's SurpRISE Mysteries

Book One

R. A. Hutchins

Copyright © 2025 Rachel Anne Hutchins

All rights reserved.

The characters, locations and events portrayed in this story are wholly the product of the author's imagination. Any similarity to any persons, whether living or dead, is purely coincidental.

Cover Design by Molly Burton at Cozycoverdesigns.com

ISBN: 9798307105955

To Old Friends
And
New Beginnings xx

Books in this Series
The Baker's SurpRISE Mysteries

Footloose and Fancy Tea
Afternoon Absentea (Spring 2025)
Fake It Till You Cake It (Summer 2025)

Other Murder Mystery Titles by this Author:
Baker's Rise Mysteries -

Here Today, Scone Tomorrow
Pie Comes Before A Fall
Absence Makes the Heart Grow Fondant
Muffin Ventured, Muffin Gained
Out with the Old, In with the Choux
All's Fair in Loaf and War
A Walk In the Parkin
The Jam Before the Storm
Things Cannoli Get Better
A Stitch In Key Lime

The Lillymouth Mysteries Trilogy -

Fresh As a Daisy
No Shrinking Violet
Chin Up Buttercup

Romances By this Author

Chasing Dreams on Oak tree Lane
Making Memories on Oak Tree Lane
Feeling Festive on Oak Tree Lane
Embracing Joy on Oak Tree Lane

To Catch A Feather – Found in Fife Book One
A Stroke of Luck – Found in Five Book Two
The Angel and The Wolf
Counting Down to Christmas
On The Doorstep
Finding Love on Cobble Wynd (Historical romance)
A Lesson in Love on Cobble Wynd (Historical Romance)

CONTENTS

Chapter One	1
Chapter Two	10
Chapter Three	18
Chapter Four	28
Chapter Five	38
Chapter Six	46
Chapter Seven	55
Chapter Eight	64
Chapter Nine	72
Chapter Ten	80
Chapter Eleven	89
Chapter Twelve	96
Chapter Thirteen	104
Chapter Fourteen	111
Chapter Fifteen	119
Chapter Sixteen	127
Chapter Seventeen	135
Chapter Eighteen	143
Chapter Nineteen	149
Chapter Twenty	160
Chapter Twenty-One	167
Chapter Twenty -Two	175
Chapter Twenty-Three	181
Epilogue	186
Excerpt from *Here Today,*	
Scone Tomorrow	193
About The Author	203
Other Mysteries by this Author	205

CHAPTER ONE

It hadn't been quite the new chapter she had imagined – rather far from it, in fact – and Naomi couldn't help but wonder if she should have taken her mum's offer after all. Of course, the feeling of returning prematurely from her patisserie training in Paris with her tail between her legs had been enough to prompt the young woman to look for a fresh start anyway, without even considering the gossip she would face back in Baker's Rise if she returned home to the village a year earlier than planned. So, she had politely declined Flora's offer of a job running the events at their family manor house, The Rise, and had instead taken the position here at Bakerslea-by-the-Sea.

A decision Naomi was now questioning as she used an

ancient bottle of white spirit found under the sink in the kitchen to scrub pale paint from her hands. Not wanting every cake she baked that afternoon to have the faint hue of 'Egyptian eggshell blue,' Naomi was becoming increasingly frustrated that the stain would not budge. When she had arrived late last night, exhausted from the train journey through the channel tunnel, and then the much slower one that brought her up to the North of England, Naomi had gone straight to her new room on the first floor – the only sense in which the room could be considered 'new', though the peeling wallpaper and chipped sink was a worry for another day – trusting that the list of supplies she had emailed ahead would be waiting in the kitchen for today's tight baking schedule. The bedroom had come with the position, and Naomi was quickly learning that if it seems too good to be true then it probably is – something she really should have learnt from her time in France.

Whilst the role here had been advertised as 'Afternoon Tea Patisserie Chef and Occasional Events Manager,' Naomi had so far spent her first morning on the job helping repaint the foyer of the old dance hall with her new upstairs neighbour, Tom. The grandson of the dance hall's owner, it seemed he had been roped in on his day off. So far there had been no sight of his grandmother, Harriet Hornsley – known far and wide as Goldie for the jewellery she always adorned herself with – which Tom had explained was normal. The older woman apparently didn't rise till midday and then took a leisurely lunch as had been her routine for years, fashioned after the late Queen Mother no less. Even now, despite the grand opening being in two days' time and the general decoration remaining incomplete even in what would be the public areas, it appeared that routine could not be changed. Goldie had left a note for them both, attached with a cat magnet to the fridge in their communal upstairs kitchen, saying that they should paint the foyer and then move onto the cloakroom. According to Tom, the professional decorators had downed tools and upped sticks the previous week in an argument over pay, leaving everywhere apart from the beautiful ballroom itself still to be painted.

As Naomi had been so keen to get back to England that she had neglected to ask for photos of what would be both her new home and workplace, she supposed she had only herself to blame. That being said, though, painting one large room had been quite enough distraction from what was supposed to be her main itinerary of the day, and even that space was only half done. Naomi had excused herself to clean up a bit, and had no intention of returning to the job, or else there would be no afternoon teas to accompany the dances that week. Surely Goldie would consider that the priority – if she ever surfaced, that is.

Never mind all that though, Naomi shook her shoulders out as if to remove the cloak of disappointment that her shrouded her since her arrival, confident that she was about to be in her happy place. With her hands scrubbed to within an inch of their life, and no time for lunch, Naomi took a deep breath in as she walked into the coolness of the large pantry, eager to begin what she had come here to do.

Naomi's eyes scanned the sparse shelves, and she bit down on the words that would have caused her late Granny Betty to tut in disapproval. Instead, Naomi couldn't help but let out what could only be described as a growl. A low noise initially which then increased in volume and note until it was almost a scream of frustration. Producing cakes and tarts which she hoped the old place would become famous for would require very specific ingredients, the very kinds that Naomi had informed her new employer of in advance, in fact, and yet there appeared to be none of her detailed requirements here. Thinking she must have overlooked a separate larder in the spacious kitchen, Naomi hurried back into the main room, randomly opening cupboard doors and drawers until she had searched the whole place. Once she had completed two rounds of the space, sweat dripping down the back of her neck in the late summer heat, Naomi finally admitted defeat, slumping down onto the large, wooden chair that stood at the head of the farmhouse style table in the middle of the room.

"Resting already? There's plenty to be done, my dear, I can give you a list," Goldie entered the room in a cloud of musky perfume and with the fluffiest cat Naomi had ever seen wedged under her arm. The creature itself scanned first the newcomer and then the room itself, whether looking for a means of escape or a tasty treat, Naomi wasn't sure.

Naomi felt her hackles rise and took a short breath, trying to temper her tone before explaining to her new boss that she had been working, very hard in fact, just not on the job she had been hired to do.

"There seems to be a delivery missing," Naomi felt short and straight to the point was best if she wasn't to launch the tirade that was bubbling up under the surface.

"A delivery?" Goldie disappeared into the pantry, emerging with a loaf of bread and heading straight for the toaster, "Carys normally prepares my lunch, but today is her day off." The older woman scrunched up her nose in displeasure as she shoved two fat white slices into the toaster, causing her ornate, dangling earrings to jangle and flash in the light from the floor length window.

Naomi had met Carys only very briefly the night before, when the kindly Welshwoman had shown her to her living quarters, and to be honest didn't really care about Goldie's normal lunch arrangements as tears pricked the back of her eyelids. She closed her eyes and tried to calm her reaction. Not normally prone to outbursts of emotion – well, not of the weepy variety anyway – Naomi blamed her sudden wobble on her current exhausted state. Perhaps jumping from one frying pan into the fire wasn't such a good idea after all.

Who knew? When will I ever learn?

Goldie was oblivious to Naomi's struggle, currently lashing jam onto the barely toasted bread as if her life depended on it. Her gold bangles shook and the cat, it seemed, had finally sensed an advantage and launched itself from the woman's arm and straight onto the table, sending a flurry of long hairs into the air. Naomi said nothing, her mouth agape and her eyes glassy as she watched the fur slowly drifting down to descend on the table, assuming Goldie would shoo the creature off what was to be Naomi's workspace. No chastisement followed, however, simply a look of maternal indulgence before Goldie finally turned her attention back to her new employee.

"Are you ill, girl?"

"Ill? No. If I were ill I wouldn't have spent all morning painting the foyer," Naomi felt the flush rise to her face as she stood, "I'm simply at a loss as to what I should bake since you don't seem to have provided any of the ingredients I requested."

"Ingredients?" Goldie had already shifted her attention back to the cat, who was now prowling the pantry.

You won't find anything tasty in there, Naomi thought to herself sardonically as she continued. "Yes, I sent an email, with a list of my requirements for this week's afternoon teas." This was not how Naomi had wanted the first proper meeting with her new boss to go, far from it in fact, and she tried desperately to control the temper that had got her into trouble more times than she could count.

"Oh, Carys does all the shopping, you'll have to give her your list, dear," Goldie said, completely unaffected by the implications of the missing items.

Does she really not understand, or does she simply not care? Naomi wondered to herself, confused. She didn't have time to query further, however, as Goldie snatched the cat up as it was about to make a dash for the door, squashing it against her ample bosom once more.

"Have you met my Ginger?" Goldie asked, thrusting the feisty feline forward and under Naomi's nose.

"Er, no, no," Naomi found herself stuttering as the bright orange fur tickled her nose and the creature gave her what could only be interpreted as a death glare.

"Ginger Pawgers, meet…"

Clearly the woman couldn't remember her name, "Naomi Bramble-Miller, patisserie chef, not painter and decorator." It was definitely bordering on rude, she knew, but Naomi's patience was down to its last thread.

"Ah yes, Naomi, the cake girl, meet Ginger Pawgers, namesake of the whole venue."

Naomi had wondered about the ballroom's name, 'Ginger's,' and had guessed it might be a tribute to the famous 1930's dancer Ginger Rogers, which she supposed it was, just rather indirectly.

"I had a Fred Pawstaire, too," Goldie continued wistfully, "but he went up to the Great Rainbow Ballroom in the sky last year."

"I'm, ah, sorry to hear that," Naomi said, wondering if the conversation could possibly get any more surreal. It was almost like being back in Baker's Rise again, but without any of the inside knowledge to be able to navigate the discussion.

"Well, let me know if you need anything, dear," Goldie said, carrying the plate of mainly jam with the toast nowhere to be seen underneath it in one hand, and the squirming cat under the other arm as she waltzed from the room.

"Oh, only about thirty or so ingredients and a will to live," Naomi muttered under her breath, picking up her paintbrush from the counter and heading back to help Tom in the entrance hall once more.

CHAPTER TWO

At least the bed was comfortable, which was a good thing as Naomi's shoulders and back ached from the painting that had taken them well into the evening. Thankfully, Tom was an amiable sort, and the time together had not been uncomfortable. Had she not sworn off men completely, Naomi might even have been swayed by either his big, brown eyes, or the skilful way his muscled arm handled a paint roller. As it was, she was completely immune to his physical charms but had certainly appreciated her new neighbour's easy-going chat and sense of humour. She had declined to share an evening meal with him, though, deciding to move past her initial annoyance and frustration and return to the main kitchen downstairs in the hope of salvaging her new role. Determined to act like the mature, mid-twenties woman she was.

Calmly this time, Naomi had made a list of ingredients that were well stocked, such as flour, butter, eggs, and – unsurprisingly – jam, and another of items which should be readily available in the local area. From these, she knew she could whip up some of the bakes from Granny Betty's recipe book which, although they wouldn't have the wow factor that some of her newly-learned Parisien pastries had, would certainly be crowd-pleasers in a small, northern town like this. With the peace of mind that came from that small task, Naomi had gone to bed ready to make a fresh start this morning.

It was a familiar sound which woke her that morning, well before her own alarm was scheduled to go off, and it brought with it a pang of homesickness that caught Naomi by surprise. Swallowing down the lump in her throat, she forced herself out of bed before the tears could fall, dragging open the heavy, damask curtains to distract herself with the view. What the old building lacked in modern amenities, it more than made up for in location, with every room on the back of the building having a magnificent view of the North Sea. It looked to be another mild September day, the waves small and the water a deep blue colour, so Naomi promised herself that after a morning of shopping and baking she would go for a walk on the beach later.

"But first, coffee," she spoke to herself as she made her way along the landing to the small kitchen-come-sitting room that was shared between herself, Tom, and Carys. Goldie had her own wing downstairs and used the main kitchen, as Naomi had found yesterday. With the older woman rising so late and baking generally being an early morning pursuit, Naomi hoped their schedules wouldn't normally overlap.

"Bonnie bird!" The unexpected squawk caught her off guard, and it took Naomi a moment to realise that she hadn't in fact been dreaming the parrot noises which had woken her.

"Be quiet, miss, it's too early for that!" Carys scolded the bird gently. "Ah, Naomi my lovey, come and have a cuppa."

The short Welshwoman reached up to take another mug from the cupboard, but it was the bird which attracted Naomi like a magnet.

"Give me a cwtch," the parrot said, a strong Welsh accent coming through on the last word. Clearly playing up to the attention, she fluffed her grey feathers and waggled her short, red tail feather enthusiastically.

"Ah, don't mind Bonnie here, she's all beak and no bark," Carys said, noting Naomi's silent contemplation of the bird.

"It's okay, I grew up with a parrot, well, from my teens anyway, and you'd almost always hear him before you saw him," the ache in her chest was back and Naomi turned quickly from the bird without allowing herself to stroke the head feathers which she knew would be soft like velvet.

"Well isn't that perfect, then? I knew we'd get on well," the older woman handed Naomi a cup of the milkiest coffee she had ever seen, yet she took it politely not wanting to cause offence. She'd have to grab an espresso in town for her morning fix of caffeine, but Naomi didn't mind, taking a seat opposite her new neighbour at the small table in the bay window overlooking the sea.

"Did you come from far then?" Carys asked, adjusting her round spectacles and pulling her dressing gown closer to ward off the draught from the old window.

"Well, yesterday I arrived from France, but I'm actually from a small village just inland from here, Baker's Rise. Have you heard of it? It's over by

Alnwick."

"Is that the one next to Witherham?"

"Yes, exactly," Naomi felt herself smiling as a cinematic reel of memories flitted through her mind, happy times in the tiny village she had learnt to call home. Once again she batted her eyelashes to be rid of the unwanted tears, reminding herself she and she alone had chosen this fresh start.

"Lovely area, that, when my late husband Gruffudd was alive he often played cricket against their teams, and I would go along with my book."

Naomi smiled, unable to speak past her emotions. You could always rely on a parrot to fill an uncomfortable silence though, she knew, and true to her species Bonnie flew over and perched on Carys' shoulder, the cage door having apparently been left wide open.

"I hope you don't mind her flying free?" Carys asked.

"Not at all, I prefer to see them in the open, having lots of space to stretch their wings," Naomi said, looking up at the bird who was now openly assessing the newcomer.

"Bonnie bird," the parrot repeated her phrase from earlier, clearly hoping for a friendly affirmation from

Naomi.

This time Naomi couldn't hold back, "Yes, you're a beautiful bird, aren't you? Look at those gorgeous feathers."

Clearly understanding at least the gist and tone of the compliment, Bonnie took that as an invitation to hop over the table and onto Naomi's arm, where she immediately began rubbing her head against her fluffy pyjama top.

"Bonnie," Carys said in what was clearly meant to be a warning tone, but which actually sounded full of love.

"She's okay," Naomi said, raising her arm to look at the bird face to face, "aren't you, Bonnie girl?"

"Bonnie bird," the little one chirped, clearly delighted with her new friend.

"What kind do you have?" Carys asked.

"Me? Oh, Reggie is my mum's parrot really, she inherited him before she adopted me. He can be… a bit of a handful. I wouldn't change him for the world, though. He's just… a real character. He's a Double Yellow Headed Amazon, mostly green but with a yellow head and some red on the tops of his wings."

"Gorgeous. Well, I've had Bonnie here for the past eighteen years and wouldn't be without her, my constant companion through good and bad," Carys said. "Now, tell me what you're planning on making for the grand opening tomorrow. Goldie tells me everything is in hand, but I'm a details woman if you know what I mean."

"Oh, absolutely I do, but I'm afraid there's not been a lot of… preparation done on the afternoon tea front before my arrival. I mean, I know you've all had your hands full and all. I just need to get some groceries really, so I'll need access to the Ginger's credit card or whatever you all use."

"Oh, I just use my pension money from the government and Goldie pays me back when she gets around to it."

Naomi didn't like the sound of that at all, but saved that conversation for her new employer, instead turning the chat to where in Bakerslea she could find the ingredients she needed. The setup here wasn't quite the professional, high-pressure environment she was used to, but then hadn't she wanted to escape all that anyway?

Naomi decided to make a conscious effort to embrace her new work-life balance, to go with the flow and see what life brought her way.

Little did she know, however, what – or rather who – was about to land on her doorstep and push that theory to its limits!

CHAPTER THREE

Naomi paused outside the once-grand manor house an hour later, turning back towards the building to take a couple of photos to send to her mum, Flora, along with the one of Bonnie the parrot which she had snapped before disappearing back to her room to get dressed earlier. She could see why the old place had appealed to Goldie as, besides from being painted a now-faded shade of dusky pink, it was very pleasing to the eye, with four large bay windows, two up and two down, symmetrically dominating the front façade. And that was before one even saw the ballroom attached to one end, forming a semi-circle of floor to ceiling length windows around the side of the building. Hugging the other end of the former manor house was a decades old glass conservatory, which Naomi had yet to investigate, but which judging by the state of its roof needed a lot of rather urgent attention. Two pointed gables marked the third storey of the building, each sitting atop one of the columns of bay windows and adding to the symmetry of the whole effect. Each of these gables housed one narrow window which Naomi assumed had perhaps once been the servants' quarters. The whole structure was simultaneously compact and imposing, and Naomi imagined the old place must have many stories to tell, its walls no doubt having seen much drama over the years. Naomi hoped there wouldn't be any new drama to add to that list, at least not while she was here, as a peaceful life was what she so desperately sought.

"Beautiful old thing, isn't she?"

The question caused Naomi to jump and swivel towards the noise. A small, stout man stood at the edge of the landscaped gardens, a long pair of cutting shears draped nonchalantly over one arm.

"Colin Chillingham, I don't believe we've met," he removed one grubby gardening glove and extended the hand towards her.

"Naomi, new patis… er, baker," she stood where she was as the gardener hurried forward, taking Naomi's proffered hand in his and shaking it vigorously.

"Ah yes, our gorgeous Goldie mentioned we would be getting a new cook, I could really do with a bacon sarnie right about now if you're…"

"I'm not," Naomi didn't mean to be rude, but this was really taking the biscuit. "Actually, I'm on my way to get supplies."

"Supplies, eh? Well, next time maybe ask around for requests first. But for now, a few packs of custard creams and some teabags – Yorkshire tea, mind, none of that weak rubbish – would be grand. Oh, and a pint of milk, full fat if you please. I live in the cottage at the far corner of the estate, follow the path around the right side of the building and you can't miss it."

Naomi attempted a smile, which didn't reach her mouth let alone her eyes, and mumbled something about being in a hurry. Saying she was pleased to meet the fellow was too much of an ask. The man didn't seem to notice, though, disappearing off towards the dilapidated conservatory with a spring in his step and whistling a jaunty tune. The last thing Naomi wanted was to be the general kitchen dogsbody, but she supposed a few extra groceries wouldn't hurt, provided she was quickly reimbursed. Her own bank account was looking rather depleted of late, and she was determined to stand on her own two feet despite the healthy bank account her parents had set up for her before she left for Paris still sitting untouched.

The walk into the small town of Bakerslea-By-The-Sea was a short five minutes down the main country road that formed part of the Northumberland coastal drive. A narrow sliver of pavement ran down one side, and Naomi imagined the path would be dangerous at nighttime what with the speed the cars were racing past her now and the lack of streetlights. A caffeine fix was the first item on her agenda for the morning. Naomi ignored the large tearoom in the market square, with its chintzy window dressings and bunting above the door, simply for the fact that she doubted it would have the strong ground coffee she was after right now. Instead, she chose the tiny café that stood just at the beginning of the paved walkway which led both to the promenade and to the beach. The gentle breeze tickled her face as Naomi paused to breathe in the salty sea air. Fresh and clean, it was almost a heady lungful, and combined with the beautiful sea view was enough to settle Naomi's frayed nerves, even if just for a moment.

Ahead and to her right, the beach spanned for at least a mile in a semi-circle shape, dotted with piles of seaweed and the occasional dog walker. To her left, a decent walk along the promenade and sitting on the headland at the end of the bay and adjacent to the sea was an ancient church, nestled next to a very modern, glass building which Naomi knew from a long-forgotten, high school trip to be the Maritime Centre. Funnily enough, the juxtaposition of old and new didn't seem out of place here, as the same was repeated all over the county. Northumberland had ancient roots and a modern outlook, and having grown up in the area Naomi didn't find the mixture of history and newness at all jarring.

The bell above the door tinkled and Naomi was hit with a strong waft of coffee as soon as she entered the small shop. Considering that a very good sign, she ventured further into the dim interior, the space lit only by strings of fairy lights around the counter, window and along the ceiling above the small seating area. At first it appeared as if the place was empty, not even a welcoming face behind the counter, until a woman of about Naomi's own age straightened from where she had been bending down behind the till.

"Oh! Hello!" The woman beamed at Naomi who immediately felt at ease. Normally, entering somewhere new and where all attention was on her immediately brought a sense of discomfort, a mild anxiety that Naomi usually tried to avoid. The welcoming expression on the other woman's face, however, and the general cosiness of the place, encouraged Naomi to approach the counter. Once she had spied the huge coffee machine against the back wall – very similar to the one in her mum's tearoom back home and which Naomi had fond memories of using – the fate of the place was sealed as her new favourite caffeine-drinking establishment.

"Hi, could I get an espresso please? Double shot, if possible," Naomi eyed the variety of delicious looking brownies in a dainty glass cabinet, "and a raspberry brownie please." A small celebration of her new chapter, she decided, once again hoping there would be no unforeseen plot twists in her near future.

"Of course, to sit in?"

Naomi hadn't intended to linger, keen to get her ingredients and head back to begin the baking process, but something prompted her to stay. She had felt lonely since arriving – well, since the moment she had set off for her grand French adventure, if she were honest with herself – and this cosy space felt like a welcoming retreat somehow, the woman behind the counter like a friend. Which was ridiculous, as Naomi had never met the barista before. Yet the feeling continued as Naomi took a seat on a banquette-for-one seat in the window, at a tiny table for two, and watched as the woman got to work, handling the coffee machine like a pro. Naomi knew from her own experience working at The Tearoom on the Rise that that particular model could be extremely temperamental, so was particularly impressed when her drink arrived after only the one attempt at making it.

"I'm Sarah, by the way, are you just visiting?"

The end of the summer season had passed a couple of weeks ago, but a few visitors still remained, milling about the place and enquiring as to which day of the week was market day. Why Goldie hadn't opened in time to catch the tourists last month, Naomi hadn't understood until she'd actually arrived at Ginger's and seen the lackadaisical way her new employer approached the business.

"Naomi, pleased to meet you. No, I've actually come to work at the new ballroom dancing and afternoon tea venue, Ginger's, in the manor house up the main road."

"The old Hadley place?" Sarah asked, her delicate eyebrows bunching together and causing her forehead to wrinkle under her thick fringe.

"I'm not sure, I haven't really read into the history

of…"

"Well, never mind, it's lovely to have someone my own age around here," Sarah smiled, though a visible tremor ran through her, and she did a little full-body wriggle as if to shake off a negative thought.

"This brownie is delicious! Did you make this?" Naomi was genuinely shocked as the gooey, chocolatey goodness hit her taste buds.

"Thank you, and yes," Sarah blushed a light pink and turned away slightly, clearly uncomfortable with the praise.

"I'm surprised Goldie didn't ask you to provide the cakes and pastries for the afternoon teas." It was a logical assumption.

"Well, she did make some enquiries locally, but no one wanted to work up th…" Sarah cut herself off suddenly, her face now a much deeper shade of red, as if she had said something she shouldn't.

Naomi felt a wave of unease come over her and downed her espresso in one large gulp.

For a moment, neither of them spoke until the shrill noise of a baby crying drew their attention. Sarah rushed over to the counter and bent down behind the till, in the same pose as she had been when Naomi arrived, though this time when she stood she was holding a little infant wrapped in a blanket.

"Couldn't afford to take much maternity leave," Sarah said as if in explanation, as she shushed the crying baby and peppered small kisses across her tiny forehead.

"She's beautiful," Naomi said, finishing the last bite of her brownie and reluctantly preparing to leave, hoping the pink blanket was a good indicator that the child was indeed a girl.

"Thank you, this is Rose," Sarah moved the blanket and came back around to the front of the counter so that Naomi could get a better look at the chubby-cheeked child.

Their eyes met briefly, hers and the baby's, and Naomi felt she could get lost in those big, blue orbs if she let herself. Her own childhood had not been a good one – not until she was fostered by the Bramble-Millers, that is – and so having a child of her own had never once seemed a viable option for Naomi. She had always doubted her own aptitude in the maternal department, seeing herself as too broken and not wanting to inflict her own emotional scars on a child. Flora and Adam, her adoptive parents, had gone a long way to healing some of that past trauma, but still having a child of her own had never been on Naomi's life bingo card of choice.

"So pretty," she said, hiding her own inner turmoil behind a smile as she was so practiced at doing, before assuring Sarah she'd be back for more of her great coffee.

"Thank you, I'll look forward to seeing you," Sarah said, and for once Naomi felt the usually throw-away platitude was genuinely meant.

CHAPTER FOUR

Naomi was very much in her own little world as she walked back up the small, tree-lined driveway which led to the landscaped gardens in front of the manor house, and so didn't notice either the familiar car parked outside or the man standing next to it. It mattered little, however, as neither would have got a word in edgewise before the shriek which emanated from inside the open car.

"My No Me! She's a keeper!"

Naomi stopped suddenly at the instantly recognisable voice, knowing immediately who it belonged to, but shocked to hear it in this place. Her eyes sought out the sound and found Adam, catching the eye roll which he directed into the vehicle through the open car door. Needing no bidding, Naomi's legs began a fast jog, ending in her father's arms.

"Dad, why are you..? How are you..?" Naomi's mind raced as the words tumbled out in breathless disarray, "Is Mum okay? Why is Reggie here?" It had only been about six months since she had left them to head for France, yet in some ways it felt like a lifetime and those pesky tears caught Naomi unawares this time and began a rapid assault on her cheeks.

Hearing his name spoken by his favourite person, the parrot began a verbal tirade, a litany of increasingly impolite requests demanding that he be removed from his travel carrier without further delay.

"Are you okay?" Adam asked, stepping back from their embrace to study his daughter's face.

"Yes, yes, just a new place, new people..."

"Aye well, you're not too far from home now to pop back and see us whenever you want, you know?"

"I know, I know. So, why is the feathery overlord here?" Naomi was sure it wouldn't just be a social visit, especially since Flora wasn't there too.

"Well, you know how your mum's just published

another of her books about Reggie? Hold on, let me get him before he screams the place down," Adam bent into the car and released the parrot, earning him neither thanks nor quiet.

"Bad bird!" Reggie labelled Adam as he burst out of the car in a flurry of feisty temper and feathers, aiming straight for Naomi's shoulder where he suddenly became all sweetness and light once again. "My No Me, Best Bird!" He rubbed his head feathers along her jawline and Naomi felt her shoulders relax slightly for the first time since leaving France.

"Love you," Reggie chirped happily.

"Love you too," Naomi whispered, using the feathery affection to dry her wet tears against her little friend's warmth. "Would you like to come inside?" She asked Adam, who looked relieved that the pair were both so happy to be reunited.

"If you don't mind, I'll just head on back. We have to be at the airport by five."

Naomi's eyes narrowed as she contemplated that information, "But Reggie hates flying – well, in planes at least."

"Exactly, which is why we knew you'd understand,"

Adam had the grace to look sheepish.

"And what am I understanding exactly?" Naomi asked, but she already had a good idea where the conversation was headed, and it really wasn't going to be possible. Not with her being so brand new here and another parrot already staking claim to the territory.

"Well, ah, your mum's recent release has become a bestseller in Australia…"

"Australia?" Naomi parroted back.

"Yes, and er, her publisher over there has arranged an impromptu book tour. Reggie was invited, of course, being the star of the stories, but after last time…"

Naomi well remembered the events in Scotland a few years ago, in particular the incident where Reggie had decided he wanted to flirt with the host's furry sporran and therefore also needed to know what was under the man's kilt. As per usual where the bird was concerned, chaos and not a small amount of embarrassment had ensued, and Flora had been mortified. Since then, Reggie had not accompanied the family on any more book publicity trips.

"I'm sorry, Dad, I simply can't, I've only just arrived and the job description seems to be a bit… fluid at the moment."

"It would only be for a few weeks, a month at most," Adam said, his eyes pleading. "I hate to do this love, but you know how down your mum's been since we lost Granny Betty, I'm hoping this'll help with the grief, you know?"

Betty had been neither Flora's biological mother nor Naomi's biological grandmother, but she had taken them both under her wing in Baker's Rise and they had become as tight as any blood family. Granny Betty had even been the one to introduce Naomi to baking when she had first arrived in the village, as a scared and life-weary thirteen-year-old. Betty's death a year prior had been the kickstart Naomi needed to put some distance between herself and the small village, lest she stay in her comfort zone running the tearoom for her parents for the foreseeable future. The grief still hit her hard at times, though, particularly when Naomi made Betty's signature bakes such as individual mini carrot cakes or cranberry fruit scones, and so she understood how Flora would need a break from the village just as she had.

Then there was Reggie himself, currently chirping away in Naomi's ear, updating her on all his news in disjointed pigeon (or parrot, in this case) English. He would be good for her soul on an emotional level, Naomi knew, but on a practical level she had no idea how such a demanding pet would fit into her as yet unknown daily routine.

"Way to lay it on thick," Naomi joked, "but yes, I know it'll be good for mum to get out of the village for a while and, to be honest, I could do with some company…" She sighed heavily, weighing up the pros and cons. The negatives won out, yet still Naomi said, "So, okay, I'll run inside and ask my new employer if I can have a pet on just a very temporary basis. If she says no, then we have our answer. You wait here."

A small struggle ensued as they tried to persuade the stubborn parrot off Naomi's shoulder, which ended with her having to do a quick duck and run whilst Adam distracted the bird with a slice of dried banana from the emergency stash in the glove compartment.

Finding no one in the main downstairs kitchen, Naomi followed the sound of samba music to the ballroom at the end of the front corridor. She had to admit, this room had been beautifully refurbished, with a polished, hardwood floor and thick, red velvet curtains dressing the tall windows from top to bottom. In the middle of the room, Goldie was currently being expertly twirled and dipped by a younger man in extremely tight clothing. Approaching them, wondering whether she should interrupt or not, Naomi inadvertently caught the dancer's eye. Up close, he looked a lot nearer to fifty than to forty, his fake tan firmly settled into the creases of his face wrinkles making him look rather like a stripy tiger given the unnaturally bright orange shade.

"And who do we have here?" He asked in a thick Italian accent, stopping mid-twirl and causing Goldie to overbalance and have to cling to him for support, which she did for rather longer than could be considered polite.

Her employer looked less than impressed with Naomi's interruption, the woman's trademark heavy gold chains jangling noisily against her bosom as Goldie tried to catch her breath.

"A glass of water, Colin!" Goldie barked to the man sitting in the shadows at one of the afternoon tea tables on the opposite side of the dimly lit room.

Naomi hadn't noticed the gardener sitting there, so still and quiet he must have been whilst watching the couple dance. *Slightly odd,* Naomi thought to herself, but aloud she jumped straight into her reason for being there, taking the drink break as her opportunity to make her request.

"Alfonso Di Campo," the man did a low, theatrical bow and rose with a flourish, his dark eyes doing a tour of her body before boring into Naomi's in such a manner that she felt immediately ill at ease. He reminded her a lot of the head chef at the patisserie kitchen back in the Hôtel du Vieux Louvre and that alone made Naomi want to get as far away from the man as she could.

"Naomi Bramble-Mill…"

"Yes, yes, the new cook," Goldie interrupted, her rings clanking against the glass Colin had just handed her. With each finger loaded with at least three, varying from ornately engraved or plaited gold bands to richly coloured jewels, there seemed to not be enough space on the woman's hand for the whole collection, which clicked against each other where they met between her fingers. "What do you need, dear? I thought I told you to direct your questions to Carys?" She spoke slowly as if to a small child.

"Cook? Ah, we'll need to have a private talk about my dietary requirements," Alfonso cut in, making Naomi like him even less, if that were possible.

"I'm a patisserie chef, not a meal maker," Naomi didn't hide the sharpness from her voice, though she tempered her tone when she spoke to Goldie, "Harriet, ah, Goldie sorry, there has been a bit of an emergency at home and I need to look after my pet bird for a few weeks, would that be okay?" It came out too quickly in her nervousness, as Naomi felt all three pairs of eyes on her, and she wondered if she should repeat herself.

Before she could begin again more slowly, however, Goldie replied, "Your living arrangements are your own affair, my dear. The rent comes out of your wages as you know, now if you don't mind, Alfonso and I were in the middle of a session."

"Si, and I must finish on the hour, sharply, as I have the Lady Mayoress next for her lesson."

Naomi caught Goldie's scowl on hearing that information, but had no desire to enquire after more details of either the dance lessons or their recipients. Between the leering Italian, whose clothes did not leave enough to the imagination, the woman adorned in gold who couldn't take her eyes off the dance tutor's lips even long enough to have a conversation, and the old gardener who, after returning to the shadows, was now taking pictures of the ballroom's owner on his phone, Naomi found the whole scene disturbing on a number of levels.

Best just to skedaddle before Goldie changes her mind…

Taking a deep breath of fresh air on the manor house steps, to combat the deeply unsettling feeling the whole encounter had triggered, Naomi hurried to Adam and Reggie, who appeared to be in a momentary standoff whilst the parrot gorged on some dried mango.

"It's settled," Naomi said, happy to see her father's face light up.

"Thank you, petal, it will be such a relief to your mum to know Reggie will be well cared for, though you can always come and birdsit at home if this place doesn't work out," he hugged her tightly and Reggie insisted on getting in on it too, landing on Adam's forearm and leaning forward to press the top half of his little body against Naomi's shoulder.

Naomi knew full well that adding Reggie into the mix was about to make her life a recipe for disaster. She knew there would be no peace and even less quiet, yet she smiled with genuine joy to have the little guy back with her once again.

CHAPTER FIVE

Naomi knew that it would be extremely foolhardy to let Reggie out of her sight, yet she had several hours of baking ahead of her, and then a team meeting which had been announced on the chalkboard in the kitchen for seven o'clock that evening, so she had no choice but to take the bird with her into the kitchen and to find him a perch on an old cookbook stand.

"She's a corker!" Reggie chirped, his beady eyes on the fruit basket in the middle of the table.

"Don't you be trying to butter me up," Naomi said, though she smiled indulgently and reached for an over-ripe banana, peeling it and then breaking it into three parts and laying it at the parrot's feet on the bench like some sort of fruity sacrifice.

"My No Me! You're my honey!" The parrot shrieked Naomi's name in delighted gratitude before grabbing one of the slippery pieces with both talons.

"Right, straight to work," Naomi spoke aloud to herself.

"To work!" The parrot echoed, spraying small bits of banana as he spoke.

There were thankfully no interruptions as Naomi found her happy zone, preparing the dough for some mini bread rolls that would be made into the sandwich part of the afternoon tea, and then making pastry for a batch of large tartes aux pommes which would be sliced for the event. Whilst the dough proofed, Naomi peeled apples – her little helper ready and willing to take the peelings off her hands – and then decided on some traditional cherry scones and mini salted caramel brownies. With some open smoked salmon sandwiches on brown bread, and her own buns filled with ham and cheese and some with egg mayonnaise, Naomi knew the offering the next day wouldn't set any hearts on fire, but they were all recipes which she could probably make with her eyes closed and so guaranteed to work out well in the very limited time she had. Once the grand opening was over, she would attempt to find her creative spark – gone awol for the past few months – and make more inventive bakes for the twice-weekly dancing teas.

Clearly the place wouldn't survive on just two events a week, so Naomi was keen to hear what else Goldie had planned, and what the baking requirements would be. Certainly, advertising the job as a 'patisserie chef' had been somewhat of a misnomer, but at least there was nothing too taxing right away and Naomi could hopefully find a better headspace without the high pressure and stress of her previous position.

The dance lessons, it seemed, continued well into the late afternoon, as Naomi could still here the music once she had finished wiping the kitchen down and scooped Reggie up from his makeshift perch to head upstairs. After his fruity feast the little parrot had been snoozing contentedly, his snores providing a gentle background hum to Naomi's work. Normally she would wear her ear pods to cancel any distractions, but today the young woman was happy to be in the moment, back where she belonged with her bird and her bakes.

Reggie snuggled instinctively against her chest, still dozing, as Naomi picked up the heavy backpack of the bird's food and belongings which Adam had left with her and made her way up the rickety old staircase to her living quarters. She had hoped to keep Reggie in her own room and then introduce the parrot to his other feathery neighbour the next day, after the grand opening, when there would hopefully be more time to make the introduction slowly and from an initial distance. As usual where Reggie was concerned though, best laid plans flew out the window as they were just nearing the top of the stairs when a shrill "Bonnie bird! Time for tea!" filled the air.

Reggie came immediately to full alert, jumping to Naomi's shoulder and gripping on tightly, his head cocked at an inquisitive angle.

"Now, Reggie..." Naomi began to warn, but as soon as another high, excited shriek reached his ears, this one barely intelligible to human hearing, the eager parrot was off with a swoop and a duck under the doorframe at the top of the landing.

Naomi had no choice but to follow quickly behind, hurrying into the kitchen to find Reggie already sharing Bonnie's perch inside the huge cage, hungrily eying the plastic trayful of seed that Carys was carrying over from the counter.

"Oh!" Carys said, shocked to find two birds where a moment ago there had just been one.

"I can explain," Naomi began, just as Bonnie and Reggie turned to face each other. For a moment there was calm as each parrot contemplated the other, before all hell seemed to break loose. Whilst one bird had the dopey look of a lovesick teenager, the other had seemingly just realised that another parrot had landed in her home and was about to steal some of her meal.

"Agh, Agh!" Bonnie shrieked, flapping her wings and hopping up and down from one perch to the next in a display of anger and aggression.

The silly green parrot opposite her, however, stood stock still, never taking his adoring gaze from the frantic flapping of her grey feathers.

It had taken a long ten minutes to persuade Reggie out of the cage and onto the wide windowsill beside the table in the bay window. In the end only a mixture of seeds, blueberries and the threat of going home to Baker's Rise had made the bird move away from the new love of his life. Bonnie had finally calmed down, other than throwing looks of disgust Reggie's way whenever she caught him in her eyeline, and after being comforted by Carys and reassured that the new bird had his own food. Naomi had been required to empty the contents of the backpack to prove that point and it had all been rather... exhausting.

"I'm sorry, I should have tried to let you know before I brought him upstairs," Naomi apologised for the umpteenth time.

"Don't worry, lovey, they've settled now," Carys handed Naomi a cup of weak tea and sat down next to her and Reggie, breathing out slowly. She still wore her cleaning apron, and Naomi wondered how the seventy-something Welshwoman had ended up here doing their housekeeping.

"Did you not think about retiring to Wales after your husband passed," Naomi had inherited Granny Betty's forthright manner, she knew, and always struggled with general chit chat and what was and wasn't socially acceptable.

Carys didn't seem bothered by the direct question, thankfully, and replied, "Not really, Goldie took me in as her housekeeper over in Morpeth when I was grieving. She needed someone to look after the place when she went on her many travels. Gave me room and board since all my savings had gone on Gruffudd's end of life care in the home. I'd known her before that, though, on the social circuit, during her marriages."

"Marriages? How many has she had?"

"Um... four I think, if you don't count the one that only lasted a day," Carys drained her teacup and admired Reggie, who was still pining next to them. "Aw I think the little fella quite fancies my Bonnie."

Naomi had tuned out her parrot's sad little chirps of protest and was very keen to hear more about Goldie's apparently colourful life, but time was not on their side as she needed to eat and change before the staff meeting. She banked the conversation for another day and offered to cook for Carys too.

"No lovey, I've had a jacket potato. There's a lasagne keeping warm in the oven for you and Tom, though, I'm not keen on that Italian pasta."

Naomi wondered if there was any other type of pasta but kept quiet on that and instead said, "You don't have to cook for me, Carys, though I'm very grateful. I did think something in here smelled delicious."

"It's no trouble, petal, I prepare each meal for Goldie so might as well make a bigger batch. I'll head down with hers now if you think you can manage both birds?"

"Oh! Yes, yes of course," Naomi replied, struggling to get her head around the fact that Goldie literally had everyone there – Naomi herself not included –

wrapped around her jewellery laden fingers. It felt a very strange dynamic, and Naomi wasn't sure what to make of it.

Not that she had time to think about that, though, as the moment Carys bent to the oven and Naomi took the two china cups to the sink, Reggie saw his chance and took it, flying over to Bonnie's cage like a bird on a mission.

This is going to be a long four weeks, Naomi thought to herself as she hot footed it across the room and manage to slam the cage door just before the determined green bird swooped inside.

"Bad bird!" Reggie squawked, clinging to the outside of the cage as if his life depended on it.

"No, you're being bad," Naomi argued back, scooping him off the railings with a quick unhooking of his talons.

"No!" Bonnie shrieked loudly, as if that was explanation enough of her feelings.

And Naomi had to agree. That was quite enough for now.

CHAPTER SIX

They were a strange group around the table in the main kitchen, to be sure. Goldie sat at the head of them all, in the spot under the tall window, her bottle-red hair shining decidedly orangey under the glow of the setting sun, matching the fur of the huge cat on her lap, whilst Colin sat to her left looking particularly officious with a notebook in a ring binder laid out in front of him. Alfonso sat to the owner's right, already appearing bored, attempting to run his fingers through his quiffed black hair which sat as stiff and upright as it had been when Naomi saw the dancer in the ballroom earlier in the day. She wondered briefly how much the man spent each week on hairsprays and gels. Not as much as on alcohol, it would seem, if the large glass of amber liquid in front of him were any indicator. Beside him sat Carys, her grey hair still in its neat bun after the day's work, and opposite her Naomi herself.

"Is Tom coming?" Colin asked Goldie, pen in hand ready to write the minutes.

"No, he texted to say his shift has run over," Goldie said dismissively, "though what can be more important than this, I do not know."

"What does Tom do?" Naomi asked, by way of joining the conversation.

"He takes photos of dead bodies," Carys said, giving no further explanation, as if that was the most natural profession in the world.

Naomi would have enquired further, but Goldie began the meeting then in a commandingly loud voice. Quite unnecessary, Naomi thought, considering they were only a few, and them all seated together around the one table.

"So, we must make this quick, I have my manicurist coming around for an emergency nail break in half an hour. As you all know, tomorrow is the day I have been working towards for months now. The pinnacle of my expert planning and provision. The grand opening of Ginger's." Colin scribbled away, hanging off the woman's every word, whilst Alfonso did nothing to hide his wide yawn as Goldie continued, "So, everything must go to plan, there must be nothing unexpected, however trifling, do you understand?"

Everyone nodded, and Naomi felt as if she had missed the whole first season of a popular new show.

"Um, would it be possible," Naomi began, almost regretting the words when every eye in the room turned to her, "um, to maybe do a quick recap for those of us who are new?"

"Naomi, dear, I see you have been cooking. Did you make anything for us to have now?" Colin said, ignoring Naomi's request entirely and eying the rows of tarts and scones covered in cling film on the counter.

"Er, no, I wasn't aware I had to…" Naomi began, just as Goldie interrupted.

"Carys, love, can you get the girl up to speed tomorrow? She seems to be struggling already."

Naomi felt her anger rise, a familiar sensation and one which she wished she had better control of being that she was now in her mid-twenties. Alas though she did not, and as her face heated beetroot red Naomi briefly wondered whether she should start with the being spoken about as if she were not even in the room, or the fact that she had not been hired as a general kitchen hand. That she was completely overqualified for that role, in fact. Then she would explain that at no point had she been given the itinerary for opening day, nor even reimbursed for buying all the ingredients for the afternoon teas, the guest numbers for which she had still to be told…

Whether for good or bad, Naomi didn't actually get to make any point at all, as Tom arrived then, his bright smile bringing with it a change in the heavy atmosphere of the room. For Naomi at least.

"Ah Thomas, there you are," Goldie said, sighing heavily, "now we can discuss the photography, which must be first class if we are to make the front pages."

Naomi, in her current bad mood, assumed a champion vegetable stall at the weekly Bakerslea market, or even a cheeky seagull stealing a sandwich on the pier would make first page news in these quiet parts, but buttoned her lips and chose to seethe quietly as the discussion took place around her. The venue was to be officially opened by the Lady Mayoress herself, no less, an old friend of Goldie's from way back, it would seem. Tom had taken a day's annual leave to take photographs of both the event and the new Ginger's members, of which Naomi had no idea how many people had already signed up. She had simply counted the number of round tables in the ballroom, multiplied that number by the amount of seats at each table – in this case, six – and used that number as her baking requirements, plus ten percent just in case.

"Colin, you're the figures man, how many memberships do we have?" Goldie barked at him.

"I thought Colin was the gardener?" Naomi whispered to Tom, who had come to sit beside her.

"And the accountant, and basically any role Goldie wants him to fulfil," Tom wiggled his eyebrows and Naomi had to suppress a snort. The first humour she had felt since arriving. "He is," Tom continued, "a bit of a lapdog. Shame Goldie only likes cats!"

Naomi laughed out loud at that point, earning her harsh glares from Goldie and Colin, and a lascivious wink from Alfonso. Naomi gave the Italian a hard stare and tried to tune back in to the dull conversation of membership tiers.

"So, as I was saying," Colin said, "for tier one we have eight members, that level entitling them to one afternoon tea dance per week. At tier two we have three members, which gets them both afternoon dances each week, and a one hour lesson with Alfonso here," his lips turned down at the mention of the dancer's name, "for tier three there is just one member so far, getting all of that plus Alfonso's undivided attention for four hours a week."

"And who is that?" Alfonso himself piped up.

"That would be the Lady Mayoress, Patricia Bonham-Smythe," Colin replied.

"And remembering also that as the owner I get all of that and more, on demand!" Goldie interrupted, her jealous streak having apparently been triggered. "And obviously the place can't run with those numbers, though I did send out dozens of invitations to tomorrow's opening, so we will need to quickly incorporate some extra events, maybe host charity galas, perhaps some wine tastings and the like. Certainly, we will need to open on Saturday afternoons and evenings for afternoon teas and maybe organise some live music for those. That is where the events managing part of your role comes in, Naomi, are you taking notes?" She ended with an exasperated sigh and a loud clanking as her heavy bracelets hit the table, where the woman started tapping irritably.

"I have the notes app on my phone open here, yes," Naomi lied, having actually been texting Flora to wish them a good trip.

"Very well then, you and Carys can begin brainstorming, I have to get off to have my nails sorted," the cat gave an annoyed yowl as Goldie hoisted the chunky creature up and half over her shoulder.

"That is the meeting ended," Colin announced officiously, as if the Queen was just departing and so now the common folk could stand and go about their business again.

Carys looked tired and Naomi suggested they leave any brainstorming until after the grand opening, earning her a smile and a rub on the back from the housekeeper.

"Yes, lovey, I think I'll be having me a long bath now. Tomorrow will be a hard one, I can feel it in my bones."

With Colin hurrying off after Goldie, that left just Tom and Alfonso in the kitchen with Naomi.

"Are you a dancer?" The Italian asked, sidling up beside her.

"No, why?" Naomi didn't turn to look at the man, already feeling the heat of him standing far too close.

"Just your figure..." He began.

"I think Goldie wanted you to go over a salsa step with her," Tom interrupted.

Naomi let out the breath she had been holding tightly, lest she scream in the dancer's face, and nodded her thanks to Tom as Alfonso hurried out of the room.

"It seems the men around here are at your grandmother's beck and call," Naomi said, when the red rage in her had calmed.

"Indeed they are, as has always been the case I believe, though I am only her grandson because she married my grandad after Granny died, so I'm probably a bit biased about the woman's ability to get her claws into people," he raised one eyebrow but said no more on the subject as they both headed upstairs.

That explains why he always refers to her as Goldie, Naomi thought to herself, *though not why he chose to take a room here.*

"Carys says you take photos of the dead?" Naomi blurted as they reached her room.

"Well, I guess that's true as I'm a crime scene photographer," Tom smiled, "not that Goldie understands that. In reality I have no experience in action shots and portraits, all of my subjects are unfortunately quite motionless to be honest," Tom gave a rue smile which exposed a dimple in his right cheek.

Naomi forced herself to look away from the cute expression, just as a loud shriek came from inside her room.

"My No Me! Mamma Mia!"

Tom looked at once shocked and then inquisitive.

"My pet parrot, Reggie, arrived today," Naomi shrugged a shoulder as if that were the most normal thing in the world.

"I'll look forward to meeting him," Tom said, and with that he was strolling down the corridor, leaving Naomi's eyes to linger on the man's retreating back.

CHAPTER SEVEN

There were two humans and two parrots for breakfast the next morning, though Naomi had chosen to sit with Reggie on the battered leather sofa in front of the empty fireplace. It was the original feature, she thought to herself, similar to those back at home in The Rise, with a black cast iron fireplace surrounded by floral, china clay tiles. Naomi had used the excuse that she was too nervous for the grand opening to eat anything, despite Carys' attempts at cajoling her to have some scrambled eggs on toast, but really she was just trying to keep Reggie away from Bonnie who was in the bay window by the table.

Reggie's portable, folding cage had been in his backpack and was now built in Naomi's bedroom, but it really wasn't suitable to keep him contained in there for more than a few hours, so Naomi knew she had no choice but to carry him around the manor house with her as she completed her daily tasks. An off-putting prospect, even without considering the fact that all the parrot really wanted to do was to get as close to his African grey counterpart as possible.

"Delivery for Naomi!" Colin's voice came from the direction of the stairwell and suddenly the issue of what to do with Reggie became decidedly more pressing. Currently scoffing a breakfast of seeds and berries, the parrot was unaware of Naomi's dilemma.

"I'll take him," Tom said, appearing from behind Naomi with a mug of coffee in one hand and a piece of buttered toast in the other. "It'll give us a chance to get acquainted." She hadn't even been aware of the man's presence in the room, but now there he was, sliding into the spot next to her on the two-seater settee, all freshly washed hair and enticing cologne.

Naomi stood up faster than she'd intended, almost knocking over her own cup which was perched precariously on the arm of the sofa, "I'll just be a minute then, thanks, he should be fine while there's food left in the bowl."

True to Naomi's word, the parrot didn't even cock an

eye as she left the room and hurried down to the entrance hall. It was quite the sight which greeted her, as Colin teetered on the top rung of an ancient wooden ladder, his hands gripping onto a huge, gilded frame which contained a portrait of Ginger the cat, complete with miniature tiara and pearl necklace.

"No, left a bit! Are you even listening?" Goldie barked, clearly not happy to be up and about before noon, as sweat dripped down the poor man's forehead. The star of the painting herself lounged on the floor at Goldie's feet, delicately cleaning herself in the way of an Egyptian queen and apparently oblivious to the commotion going on above her head.

Naomi acknowledged the beautiful picture, whilst actually thinking quite the opposite, and grabbed the box which lay on the antique console table to the side of the double front door. She hadn't been expecting anything, having not had a chance to register her new address anywhere yet, and so was curious to see what the package might be. It didn't take long to discover, however, as on closer inspection the box itself was decorated with cutely painted bees and the label 'Three B's Bakery – Bakerslea Beans and Bites.' Each 'B' in the name was decorated with a little bee, and Naomi loved the branding.

She paused outside the kitchen to read the note inside which simply said, "**Good luck on opening day, love from Sarah and Rose xx**"

"Aw that's so lovely," Naomi spoke aloud to herself as she pushed open the kitchen door to be met with pandemonium. The box of brownies was quickly forgotten in her haste to grab Reggie, who was currently sitting on Tom's head, whilst the man himself was standing by the sink scrubbing coffee off his clean chinos.

"Bad bird!" Reggie screeched when he saw Naomi, clearly unhappy at being left with the stranger. Tom, it seemed, had borne the brunt of that anger, though, and Naomi felt awful.

Carys was fussing over Tom, trying to wipe his trousers with a dishcloth, as he batted her hand away from his crotch whilst, clearly unsettled by the whole incident, Bonnie shrieked and flew around the room in circles.

"Reginald parrot!" Naomi said, scooping the bird up and apologising on repeat to everyone else in the room.

Finally, peace reigned once more, as Naomi stood at the window trying to distract Reggie with the sea view. The waves were nowhere near as calm today, crashing onto the shore in a tide of white foam. The parrot himself, however, was facing quite the opposite direction, back into the room, and was tracking Bonnie's every movement as Carys calmed the bird by snuggling her against her apron.

"Perhaps it would be better to get them used to each other rather than trying to keep them apart?" The Welshwoman suggested, for now keeping a safe distance on the other side of the room whilst Tom had disappeared to change his trousers.

"I think you might be right," Naomi agreed, turning to face her again.

"Bonnie, this is Reggie," Carys said as she walked very slowly towards them, her parrot on her hand now. "Reggie this is Bonnie," she continued, "Bon-nee, Bon-"

"Bon-bon!" Reggie squawked, very happy with himself. "Bon-bon, My Bon-bon. She's a keeper!"

"No, not yours," Naomi whispered, though she knew her feathered friend was ignoring her.

The grey parrot said nothing, hiding her face in the crook of Carys' arm, though Naomi was relieved to spot that every few seconds Bonnie would quickly peek out, take a look at Reggie and then hide again. The peeking became bolder and began to last a good couple of seconds, giving hope that the bird might actually accept Reggie in her space by the end of the week.

Half an hour later, Naomi checked her outfit in the full-length mirror in her wardrobe for one final time before encouraging Reggie onto her shoulder to go down to the kitchen. She had decided to keep him in there with her for the morning, and then return him to his cage in her room before guests began to arrive for the official opening at one o'clock. The stress had already begun to take its toll, as evidenced by the much-depleted contents of the brownie box, with Naomi having 'tasted' at least four. Salted caramel, raspberry, millionaire's and blondie were the ones to have already disappeared in a binge of nerves, with Naomi declaring them the best she had ever tasted. Even better than her own. She made a mental note to see if Sarah would like to bake a few batches for Ginger's, though that was dependant on Goldie paying for the ingredients Naomi had already bought and also guaranteeing she'd stump up for any outsourced bakes. Sighing heavily, Naomi made her way downstairs, knowing that having any such conversation with her employer would be extremely difficult. Certainly, today was not the day to ask for clarification on anything that wasn't immediately required.

The noise level increased as Naomi reached the foyer, with Colin now hanging a deep red velvet curtain over the pet portrait, a long, golden cord hanging down to one side. His portable radio sat on the floor emitting a loud string of international cricket scores, whilst Carys polished all of the glass in the entrance around him, singing away to herself as she worked.

Sidestepping that room entirely, Naomi hurried down the corridor to the kitchen, always her refuge in any location. Sadly, on this most auspicious of occasions, the peace she sought was not to be found here either.

"The fool has arrived," Reggie screeched upon seeing Alfonso, the man himself red-faced at the large range cooker, a pan of sizzling bacon sending fat and hot oil spraying back up into the man's face. "Here comes the jerk!"

"Reggie!" Naomi scolded, wishing she could just scoot back upstairs and hide in her bedroom.

"Ah Naomi, why is there no breakfast provided on this most important of days? I come in, expecting to see, how you say it? A full spread. And nothing! Niente!

Not even a warm blueberry muffin or a cheese omelette to satisfy a man's hunger when he is to be active all day! I'm a physical worker, you know, I need my body to…"

Naomi cut him off there, "I'm here to make the cakes and breads, Alfonso, the pastries and pies, not to serve three meals a day. You'll need to take it up with Goldie." Exasperated, and trying to hide the fact that her heart was beating wildly in her chest from the confrontation, Naomi let Reggie fly free to his little perch across the room, secretly happy to see the Italian have to jump out of the bird's path.

"Would you be asking Goldie anything today, signora? Have you seen the temper she is in? And what is this green bird? Mio Dio, this place gets madder by the day. I bet this parrot has had his breakfast, si?"

Naomi let the man have his say as she pottered about, retrieving the vintage china cake stands she had found in a cupboard and setting them out on the long, wooden table in rows. Eventually, Alfonso's blustering faded out as he slammed the bacon between two slices of untoasted white bread and stormed out, even forgoing a plate.

Naomi was relieved to see the dancer go and shut the heavy door quietly behind him.

"Right Reggie," she said, stroking the bird's soft yellow head as the parrot himself added "Good riddance!" for good measure. "Right Reginald, enough heckling, let's get to work, shall we?"

Naomi's tone was positive, but inside a certain panic had begun to build and she began to wonder if heading back to Baker's Rise after this event might not be the better option.

CHAPTER EIGHT

As the guests began to arrive, Naomi kept herself busy filling the cake stands in the kitchen, wanting everything to be as fresh as possible. She was half regretting her choices now, but it was too late to change anything so the afternoon teas would be served with everything she had baked the day before. Reggie was snoozing happily upstairs after a huge lunch of broccoli, carrots and corn. Taking pity on her small new housemate – though she knew the parrot's behaviour had in no way earned it – Naomi had spent her own five minute coffee break ordering a proper cage for the bird and two tall perches, telling herself that he would likely be coming to visit her wherever she was in the future anyway, so the items would be well used.

Carys rushed between the kitchen and the ballroom, ferrying glasses and cutlery, napkins and centrepieces, which she produced from a cupboard in the far corner of the kitchen that Naomi hadn't even known existed, being as the wood of the narrow door blended perfectly with the heavy shutters on either side of the original, draughty window. The views were gorgeous, the temperature inside anything but, so Naomi had ensured the range was warm all morning to keep them both comfortable as they worked. Several beautiful vintage tea sets followed from the cupboard, which seemed to be the storage equivalent of Mary Poppins' carpet bag, and then some stylish, art deco, silver-plated coffee pots. The items reminded Naomi so much of her mum's inherited china back at The Rise, that she had to stifle another unsettling bout of homesickness.

Thankfully, the situation at hand was distraction enough. Each time the door opened from Carys' toing and froing, Naomi caught blasts of conversation as Goldie loudly welcomed guests with an offering of flutes of champagne in the foyer. The venue's owner was required to repeatedly explain that they all needed to wait there for the grand unveiling, whilst most of the new arrivals seemed keen to get on with the dancing.

Unveiling what? Naomi wondered briefly, until she remembered the huge portrait of Ginger with its velvet curtain, and everything became clear.

She would have been quite happy to hide there in the kitchen, ensuring the afternoon teas went out on time when the guests sat down, had Colin not poked his head around the door five minutes later and insisted that Naomi join everyone on the front steps to await the arrival of the Mayoress.

Blinking in the low winter sun, and feeling the chill after emerging from the warm kitchen, Naomi wished she had thought to put a cardigan over her standard work attire of smart black blouse and trousers. She stood at the top of the entrance steps, trying to hide in the doorway, whilst the other staff members took more prominent positions on the stairs. To her left, Goldie dazzled in a thin, satin dress in bright fuchsia, the unforgiving material clinging to her voluptuous curves, and the grumpy cat draped around the back of her shoulders like a stole. Every so often the creature would lose its grip on the slippery material and would scrabble with its claws to get a better footing. Naomi dreaded to think what state the satin would be in by the end of the event. Beside Goldie, Colin stood in a full tuxedo, complete with a bow tie in the same material as his employer's dress, mopping his brow with a cotton handkerchief and trying but failing to direct his eyes anywhere but at Goldie's cleavage. Below them, the invited guests assembled in a fussy crowd, though they were a decidedly smaller congregation than Naomi had envisaged. Goldie, too, must have been unimpressed by the numbers, since Naomi spotted her boss doing repeated headcounts with her index finger pointed toward the group, as if they were all on a strange school trip. These numbers were then muttered to Colin, with much head shaking and jangling of heavy ruby earrings, whilst the small man himself simply nodded his head silently, not wanting to fuel the woman's ire further no doubt.

A couple of steps below Naomi stood Alfonso, in his trademark skintight trousers which he had now paired with a billowing, fuchsia satin shirt, unbuttoned almost to the waist and exposing a thick crop of salt and pepper curls. Naomi scrunched her face in distaste, but alas not before the Italian had seen her looking. He quickly stubbed his just-lit cigarette out on the black iron handrail next to them and began a slow shuffle with his feet, causing the man's narrow hips to gyrate as he raised his arms as if caressing an invisible dance partner. The movement, combined with the lascivious wink he sent her way, caused Naomi to shrink further back behind the door, next to Carys who must've been exhausted after finally finishing her preparations, and who had quickly changed into a fuchsia blouse and a fresh, frilly white apron. It seemed that only Tom and Naomi herself hadn't got the hot pink memo, not that she minded at all having every intention of hiding in the kitchen for the rest of the event.

Tom stood at the foot of the concrete staircase, a multipocketed, leather bag over his shoulder and all ready with a professional camera in hand. Next to him on the gravelled driveway, and perhaps the most surreal element of the whole welcome committee, was a Salvation Army brass band, currently playing show tunes, with their donation pot on the ground in the middle of their neat semi-circle.

I hope Goldie has made a generous contribution, Naomi thought to herself, whilst knowing that was not at all likely to be the case.

Finally, after what felt like too many repeats of 'Memory' and 'Think of Me,' Naomi spotted a white limousine pulling onto the driveway and making its way up the tree-lined avenue, bordered on either side by the landscaped gardens. An audible sigh of relief rippled through the small crowd as Goldie pushed past Colin and began barking, "Camera at the ready, Thomas!"

Tom, of course, was already poised to take the first shots of the woman exiting the impressive vehicle, as the car pulled up horizontal to the group and a short, bald man heaved himself out of the driver's seat and dawdled around to open the passenger door which faced the onlookers.

"Get a move on, man!" Goldie hissed, hopping up and down from one foot to the other and causing her belt made from a single row of pearls to jump up and down on her stomach.

An anticipatory hush came over the small gathering as they waited for the Mayoress to exit the vehicle. As the seconds passed, however, quick whispers began to emerge, some saying they hadn't even been aware that such a tiny town as Bakerslea-By-The-Sea had a mayoress, and would she be wearing a hat do you think, and others wondering if Alfonso had a dance card. Studying them now, Naomi saw that most of those in attendance were women, though a few suited and booted men stood among them, looking thoroughly bored.

A small noise caused Naomi to shift her attention back to the long car, where Tom was kneeling in front of the open passenger door, camera pointed to get the first glimpses of the guest of honour emerging, the view as yet blocked by the rear end of the chauffeur. At the man's request, Goldie too was now peering inside the back of the limo, with the noise Naomi had heard having risen to a shriek which emanated from the older woman like a banshee's cry.

"Pattie! Pattie love, wake up!" Goldie managed to back out of the car to ask for help before her shrill, keening sound resumed. "Thomas! You work with dead people, check for a pulse!"

In her panic, though, she hadn't thought to be slightly more discreet and so a loud gasp arose from the crowd, which surged forward for a better look, blocking the way for Colin who was desperately trying to get to the front and restore a sense of calm.

"Now, now, everyone, let's just…" the man began, stopping when it quickly became clear that no one was going to listen.

"Ooh, what do you think has happened?" Carys asked standing on her tiptoes and still only reaching about five feet tall.

"Perhaps she's just fainted," Naomi gave what she hoped was a reassuring smile.

"Stuff this, I need a stiff drink," Alfonso pushed rudely

past both women and disappeared towards the ballroom.

All eyes were on Tom as he backed out of the car and turned to Goldie, whom Colin had managed to silence with a quick mention of profits and reputation.

Quiet now reigned, save for a squeak from a slippery trumpet as Tom gave his verdict.

"I think she's dead."

CHAPTER NINE

Ah ambulances and police sirens, the familiar sounds of home in Baker's Rise, Naomi thought sardonically as she hand washed the china cake stands in the deep butler sink. Strictly speaking, it was Carys' job and not hers, but the older woman had been as white as a sheet since the discovery of the body and so Naomi and Tom had offered to do the clearing up, encouraging the housekeeper to lie down upstairs. Simply to help out, you understand, not at all because a detective was due to arrive at any moment to interview the limousine driver, who currently sat next to them at the kitchen table, his third cup of Earl Grey with milk and three sugars sitting in front of him. Sweat pooled on the man's baldpate and under his arms, dampening the shirt that was stretched taut over his beer belly. Both Naomi and Tom were keen to hear how the man hadn't noticed his passenger was dead. It had seemed rather rude to ask him directly, given the shocking circumstances and all, so they were trusting the detective would do it for them whilst they subtly eavesdropped from the other side of the room. Presumably the poor woman's death had been from natural causes, but the police officer in charge had thought the case suspicious enough to call one of the detective squad, so they might as well get the information straight from the horse's mouth, so to speak. No doubt Goldie would be demanding answers soon enough.

As regards the grand opening of Ginger's, sadly the string quartet had been sent home from the ballroom without playing so much as one run through of 'Blue Danube,' the grand feline portrait remained hidden behind its regal curtain, and Goldie had rushed off to her quarters the moment the body had been driven away, citing a migraine attack and insisting Alfonso mop her aching brow. The local police had allowed the guests to go home, since none had been in the car or even in the manor house that day, therefore it could be safely assumed they had had no recent contact with the deceased. Having offered to sit with Goldie in her rooms and been robustly refused, a red-faced Colin had told the police he would be in the gardener's cottage if they needed him, had checked that the limo driver was being looked after, and had then to all intents and purposes disappeared.

This all conspired to mean that the old place was suddenly very quiet. Not that Naomi was complaining. For the first time that day, she felt she could breathe properly. Tom had an easy, quiet way about him that was at once a comforting presence whilst also not intruding on one's own thoughts. A talent few possessed, Naomi had come to realise in her two and a half decades of life. Tom didn't try to fill the silence with chatter, didn't try to solve her problems, didn't have any expectations or ulterior motives. A breath of fresh air, indeed.

The soothing sound of silence was soon broken however, as is always the case, and not for the first time it was a loud, green parrot to blame. The portable cage was only effective whilst the bird was asleep, it would seem, as they heard the little Houdini coming down the stairs looking for Naomi before they saw him.

"My No Me! Bad Bird! All shook up! Mamma Mia!"

"There was a time some builders taught him Elvis song

lyrics and another event that had an Italian theme," Naomi felt herself blushing at the parrot's rather eclectic range of vocabulary, whilst Tom simply chuckled at her explanation.

"Reginald parrot!" Naomi met him in the hallway, "Why are you not upstairs? Out of the cage is fine, but stay in the bedroom please. I have work to do."

"You're a corker!" The parrot replied landing on her arm, and Naomi was in no doubt he was trying to butter her up for a second lunch. She had no choice but to take him into the kitchen with her, lest he squawk the place down and wake Carys.

"Strange place, this," the driver – whom they could tell by his name badge was called Tony – said. His first words since the local constable had deposited him in here to wait for further questioning.

Perhaps the sugar has finally kicked in, Naomi wondered as she saw both man and bird eying up the plates of scones that had gone uneaten. All of the cake stands had been emptied and the baked goods placed in Tupperware boxes or on covered plates.

"Pointless letting it all go to waste, I suppose," Naomi angled her comment at Tom, seeking his approval as the owner's grandson – however tenuous that link actually was.

"Agreed," Tom nodded decisively, drying the last of the china stands and placing it gently on the counter. "I'm starving, let's eat."

And so that's how the detective found them, two very different men, one frazzled woman, and a feisty bird, all sitting around the kitchen table up to their beaks in cream scones and Earl Grey tea.

"Hello? The front door was still open, so I let myself in," a tall, dark-haired man poked his head around the kitchen door.

"Come in," Tom stood, hastily wiping the jam from the corners of his mouth with the back of his hand.

"Detective Timpson, here to follow up on the unfortunate death earlier," the man did a quick scan of the room, barely pausing on the parrot as if that were quite a normal animal to find. Or, more likely perhaps, the detective had simply seen so much in his career to shock, that very little did any more.

Now, one thing about Reggie that couldn't be denied, he never forgot a face. Regrettably, that was the case now as the parrot started hopping along the chair back he had been using as a perch, bobbing up and down agitatedly.

"The fool has arrived! Watch out, hide it all! Secrets and lies!" The rude parrot squawked, seemingly on a roll.

"I'm so sorry," Naomi immediately rose, tapping the bird's beak to encourage him to button it.

The detective didn't seem at all offended, instead cocking his head to one side and studying Naomi with a searching gaze.

"Do I know you?" He asked.

"I d-don't think so, I've only just moved here," Naomi didn't know why she suddenly felt so anxious, but she could feel her face and neck heating under the man's scrutiny.

"And before that?" He asked.

"Um, France, ah briefly, but mainly Baker's Rise, a small villa…"

"Yes! That's it! You're Adam's daughter, and this must be Reggie," he seemed rather less enthused by the bird as with the young woman, casting a brief, wary glance at the parrot before continuing. "Detective Timpson, I took over from your father when he retired, just around the time you came to live with them, I think? Worked with your dad's former partner, McArthur, for a few years until my promotion. Baker's Rise was like my second home back then, always something happening."

"Yes, yes, I remember now," Naomi said politely, though the man before her now bore barely any resemblance to the nervy, young investigator she had been acquainted with back then. Besides, Naomi had been in her early teens, and Timpson probably at least a decade older, so not really on her radar at all.

"Well, no time for reminiscing now, you must be the chauffeur I suspect?" Timpson turned his attention to Tony, his voice returning to an altogether more formal tone as he eyed the man who had taken advantage of the previous conversation to help himself to another scone.

Unaware of, or perhaps not bothered by the cream and jam stuck to his chins, the driver proceeded to answer all of Timpson's quick-fired questions whilst Naomi and Tom made a pretence of preparing cups of tea for them all.

A policewoman, who must have slipped into the room unnoticed, stood behind the detective and took notes, whilst Reggie scoffed the scone pieces he had been given as a bribe to keep the bird quiet.

CHAPTER TEN

"So, just to recap," Timpson said, looking sternly at the deceased woman's driver, "Mrs. Bonham-Smythe was waiting impatiently on the front steps to her home when you arrived. You were a few minutes late as you had to drop your granddaughter at nursery. She's ah, in the afternoon class. Very good." He paused to accept the cup of tea which Naomi placed on the table in front of him, before continuing, "Thank you. Yes, so the deceased was impatient and had a lot to say about your tardiness, so was clearly in full spirits as she entered the car. You had no concerns for her health at all. As the journey started she began coughing slightly. This model of car has no divider between the driver and the passenger. As Mrs. Bonham-Smythe had previously told you in no uncertain terms not to regard her from the rearview mirror, you did not look to check she was okay, fearing a further chastisement. After another few minutes, the lady asked you to pull over so she could find her asthma inhaler in her bag and take that. To give her privacy, you stepped out of the car, were distracted by a column of mother duck and ducklings and so snapped a picture on your phone to show your granddaughter later."

He paused to speak with the policewoman, who made a note to check the time stamp on that picture and requested Tony's phone. The driver handed it over without hesitation, and the summary began again as Naomi shared a look of mutual agreement with Tom. The pair slid back into their original seats, cups of tea in hand, and ready for part two.

"So, ah, you re-entered the car, took the lack of coughing as a sign that the inhaler had done its job, and drove away. You noticed nothing untoward in your passenger's posture as you took your seat and were, ah, keen to get the hoity-toity woman deposited and off your hands," Timpson made air quotation marks with his two index fingers to indicate he was quoting the chauffeur directly then. "So, you arrive, see the welcome committee assembled outside, come around to open the passenger door, and find the lady upright but with her head lolling forward. You ask Harriet Hornsley to ask after the woman's wellbeing, as you didn't want, ah, another earbashing as you put it. Then Thomas Hornsley, here, was asked to check for a pulse. I presume you are a relative of the aforementioned Harriet?"

"Me?" Tom asked, suddenly realising all eyes were on him. He looked like he had been daydreaming, his gaze fixed on the table. "Ah, only by marriage. My grandfather, Barnaby Hornsley, was her fourth husband, only very briefly. He passed three months after the marriage, about a year ago, and ah, unexpectedly left Goldie this manor house in his will. Up until their relationship, the place had been slated to go to my father."

"Pardon me for the interruption, but ah, I'm a bit lost now. Who is Goldie?" Timpson's brow had erupted in furrows of confusion.

"Harriet's nickname, because of all the jewellery she wears," Naomi filled in.

"Yes, since way before my grandad met her, I think," Tom continued. "Everyone knows her as that. Anyway, I guess she gave me the room here rent free to kind of make amends or something? Certainly, it did nothing to temper my father's anger on the subject but, ah, I digress. Basically I'm really living here so I can feed back to my dad anything unusual, or whatever, to help his legal case to contest the will, but I'm keeping up my agreement to give her free photography when she needs it so as not to arouse her suspicion. That's why I was waiting for the car with everyone else. Grand opening day photography duties."

"I see, so is Mrs. Hornsley legally allowed to go ahead and set this new venue up then? What with a legal contestation underway and all?" Timpson asked.

"Put it this way, no one has been able to stop her," Tom replied, unable to hide the bitterness in his tone.

"And you are a professional photographer?" Timpson queried.

"Forensic, yes."

"Ah, I thought I recognised you. Must've been at a few crimes scenes together. So many familiar faces here," Timpson's mouth managed a half smile as he looked around the room, landing on Reggie, who was now on Naomi's shoulder accepting her head rubs magnanimously, where the smile disappeared.

"I have the shots I took as the car door was opened, if they are any help," Tom offered.

"Hold onto them until we see whether it was foul play, but yes, thanks, and I believe it was you who checked for a pulse? Did anything strike you as odd about the body?"

"It was. Couldn't find one, checked again a few times whilst Colin called an ambulance. Only odd thing I noticed was that the lady appeared to have suffered a nosebleed, though not a substantial one, just some smearing around her nose and mouth."

"Interesting, thank you. And Colin is?" Timpson asked.

"The ah, gardener, accountant, he has lots of hats," Naomi replied, sensing Tom was done with the whole conversation if his heavy sigh was anything to go by.

"And where can I find him? And this Goldie?"

"Colin will be in the gardener's cottage and Goldie in her rooms off the ballroom, back of the building downstairs. Though she seems to have come down with a migraine." Naomi shrugged her shoulders causing Reggie to fly into the air, his eyes fixed on Timpson.

"Right well, I'll seek them out," the detective said, scraping his chair back and hurrying to the door, his eyes on the parrot. "Tony, thank you for your help. You can go home for now, though you'll need to come into the station to give an official statement tomorrow. Ask one of the constables to give you a lift home as the car has been impounded for forensic testing."

"What? But that's my livelihoo…" the driver began, but Timpson had already left.

"That little sleep was just what I needed, shocking thing wasn't it? Though I could feel it in my bones something bad was going to happen, and I'm rarely wrong," Carys said later that evening as the three of them sat in the upstairs kitchen and tucked into some of the sandwiches that had been meant for the afternoon teas. Carys had already tut-tutted that they were having Earl Grey tea with the makeshift dinner, as apparently she had planned to serve Lady Grey to their guests – much more fitting for the flavours, the amateur tea connoisseur assured them.

"It was awful, but likely nothing to worry about," Tom said, smiling reassuringly. "Most likely natural causes."

"How old was the Mayoress? I didn't get a look at her." Naomi asked.

"Well into her sixties, I'd say, and I'm not one to gossip, but I've heard her husband is much older," Carys leaned forward and affected a stage whisper.

"Retired banker in his eighties, has no inclination for dancing of any kind, so encouraged her lessons with Alfonso, so I've heard. The ladies at my knitting circle also reckon Patricia – may she rest in peace, of course – was just like Goldie. Two peas in a pod, in fact, rumour has it they knew each other from way back. Apparently Patricia's third husband had been Goldie's second, and there may have been some crossover, if you understand my meaning. Not that I'd ever gossip though."

"Of course not," Tom reassured her as Naomi spotted the wry grin he tried to hide behind his next bite.

"Both women are mutton dressed like lamb, if you ask me, I don't know what men see in them, my Gruffudd always preferred the natural look," she paused to smooth back her grey hair, her eyes suddenly glassy, "and that Patricia was as much a mayoress as I'm the Queen of Sheba!"

"Really?" Naomi asked, intrigued.

"Yep, styled herself as a lady mayoress just because she and the husband run the town's rotary club. Like Goldie, it seems no one would stand up to her. Anyway, things should be quiet around here for a few days, as that woman's migraines are a thing of legend. Never last less than thirty-six hours," Carys informed them.

As if to prove her wrong, on the quiet front at least, Reggie chose that moment to finish his blueberries, the remains of which were now stuck to the seed husks that also adorned his face feathers.

"Best bird!" he eyed Bonnie who was still finishing her fruit on the opposite side of the bay window nook, the table of adults between them. "My Bon-bon!"

"This is Reggie," Carys told her own parrot, noticing the bird still refused to look at Reggie directly, though thankfully she had stopped shrieking whenever she saw him. "Reg-gee."

"Big Gee" Bonnie suddenly squawked, causing Tom to snort.

"You're making him sound like a rapper," he said to the little bird who, enamoured by the man's attention, found the courage to shuffle closer to him along her perch.

"Reg-gee," Carys repeated patiently.

"Best bird! Ooh sexy beast!" Reggie appeared to be praising himself this time, his little chest fluffed to its fullest.

"Edgee," Bonnie tried again, and they all laughed.

"Good enough," Naomi said, grateful for the light relief after such a heavy day.

CHAPTER ELEVEN

The next morning was the first time that year that it had truly begun to feel like autumn. A strong wind blew in from the sea, causing the old building to rattle and creak whilst Naomi busied herself in the main kitchen, wondering what to do with all the leftover food. In the end, with no one to tell her otherwise, she packed it all up and phoned a local retirement home to see if they would like an afternoon tea. Delighted and offering to come straight round and collect it, the centre's manager assured Naomi it would make their residents' day.

Satisfied that nothing would go to waste Naomi retreated back upstairs, found the business card in yesterday's empty brownie box, and called Sarah to thank her for the thoughtful gift. The sound of little Rose crying formed the background to their brief conversation, so the women agreed to meet that evening for a proper chat and to get to know each other better.

"I live above the Salty Sea Dog, do you know it? It's on the main street, opposite end of town to you though."

"I don't, but that's not a problem. I don't mind the walk."

"Perfect, would after seven be okay? Then I can get Rose down. I help my mother-in-law in the bar most nights, but I'll tell her I'd like a couple of hours off tonight."

"As long as your, er, husband, or um… partner won't mind?"

The question was followed by an uncomfortable pause.

"It's just me and Kath, our Jamie passed away before Rose was born."

"I'm so sorry Sarah, I shouldn't have assumed…"

"Not at all, I did call her my mother-in-law after all, it's just still a bit raw. Anyway, looking forward to tonight, shall we get pub grub?"

"That'll be perfect, see you then."

Naomi hung up feeling very unsettled and wishing she'd learnt to rein her big mouth in. She didn't have long to dwell on it though, as no sooner had she made the resolution to unpack and properly hang up her clothes – currently half in her case and half strewn about the room, as if their owner wasn't yet sure she was staying – than the air was filled with a bloodcurdling scream.

With Tom at work, and Carys gone into town to buy some vegetables to make a hearty soup for them all, Naomi knew it was down to her to investigate. Well, her head knew this, but her feet appeared to think they were stuck in thick mud, so reluctant were they to move.

"All shook up! Pipe down!" Reggie shrieked, startled awake as the screeching sound from below them was repeated.

"It's okay," Naomi hurried to his perch to stroke the little bird's head, encouraging him onto her shoulder, her feet happy to be moving in the direction opposite the door.

Heavy footsteps could be heard charging up the stairs and a heavy knock landed on the bedroom door. Real anxiety had set in now, and Naomi stood frozen to the spot, tapping Reggie's beak to keep the parrot quiet as her own breathing came in quick gasps.

"Naomi, it's Colin, are you home?"

"Ah, y-yes," Naomi's voice faltered as she struggled to make herself loud enough to be heard. "Yes, come in."

"We need your help downstairs, all hands to the pumps, do you know where Carys is?"

"Out shopping, I think."

"Well, you'll have to do. Ditch the bird and get down there will you?"

Naomi heartily objected to being ordered around, and ordinarily would have said so, but this time simply nodded, ripples of fear still bouncing around inside her chest. As an act of defiance, though, she kept Reggie with her as she descended the stairs.

The screams, it seemed, had now descended into ragged sobs and it was a distraught Goldie that Naomi found in the entrance hall. The older woman was barely recognisable in plain, black silk pyjamas and without her usual heavily made-up face or weighty jewellery. She clutched Alfonso to her, squashing the dancer's face against her own wet one. The Italian himself gave Naomi a look which screamed 'save me,' but Naomi directed her questions to her boss instead.

"Goldie? What's happened?" Naomi asked.

The woman merely shook her head in apparent desolation and began howling again.

"Bad bird! Silly old trout!" Reggie declared, before quickly hiding himself in Naomi's cardigan to avoid the older woman's wrathful glare.

"Is it the death, has it just hit her?" Naomi questioned Colin instead, hoping to get more sense out of the man who was currently rubbing circles on Goldie's back and trying to prise her off Alfonso.

"Considering you don't live here, you always seem to be around just when there's trouble, don't you?" Colin spoke to the other man, and was about to answer Naomi when Goldie herself spoke up again.

"My Ginger, my poor baby! How could I?" She clutched her head dramatically, as Alfonso saw his moment and took it, sidestepping the woman's body and hurrying to the open doorway for a breath of fresh air.

"Mamma mia! Mio Dio!" The Italian exclaimed, and a muffled little "Mamma mia" came from Reggie parroting the words back to him.

Naomi smiled down at the bulge in her cardigan where the bird hid and asked gently, "What has happened to Ginger?"

"Gone!" Goldie shrieked, throwing herself at Alfonso once again, who staggered backwards under the onslaught.

"It seems that when Goldie bent to check the lady in the limousine, that Ginger jumped from her shoulders. In all the melee, no one noticed the cat was missing until… well, now," Colin whispered the last bit, clearly not wanting to trigger Goldie further.

"It was the blasted migraine, and the shock of it all, seeing the dead body like that," Goldie's lip quivered, and she looked desperately to Alfonso to kiss it better. This prompted the Italian to suddenly remember a dance lesson he was meant to be giving, so he made his excuses and prised Goldie's ringless fingers off his arms, quickly exiting the scene. Colin, though, was more than happy to take the man's place, moving to encourage Goldie into his own embrace.

"Get off me, Colin, I don't need to be comforted, we need a search party, you fool!" Goldie snapped, her demeanour changing in an instant.

The woman didn't notice the hurt look Colin gave her, or how it morphed into anger, but Naomi did, just as the little parrot snuggled against her echoed, "You fool!"

CHAPTER TWELVE

Naomi always felt uncomfortable walking into bars and restaurants alone, her anxiety often getting the better of her. Thankfully, however, the Salty Sea Dog was a welcoming place filled with warm lamps and kitsch seaside memorabilia. On one side of the room, a large dog slept on a rug beside the open fire.

Sarah spotted her immediately, as she served a nearby couple, "I'll be right with you."

Naomi nodded and gave a little thumbs up sign, scanning the room for a free table. Her eyes soon landed on a familiar figure in the corner.

"Detective Timpson, it's good to see you again,"

Naomi smiled down at the man who was engrossed in his phone, wondering if she shouldn't have said anything as she took the free table next to him.

"Hmm? Oh! Ms Bramble-Miller, hello."

"Please call me Naomi."

"Will do," he smiled, the expression softening his angular features and drawing attention to the man's eyes which, though their hazel colour was striking in itself, were most prominent for their inherent sadness. Naomi recognised the almost-hidden emotion, having seen it looking back at her in the mirror for the first decade and a half of her life, and wondered what had happened in the intervening years since they first met in Baker's Rise to cause the man such sorrow. As far as Naomi remembered, Timpson had always been a happy chap, if rather naïve.

"How is the post mortem going, have you heard anything yet?" Naomi asked, sticking to a safely neutral subject. Besides, she was Flora's daughter after all, and always keen to get the details.

"Well, ah," he seemed to be considering how much to share before apparently making a decision and lowering his voice," yes, unfortunately the death was not from natural causes. The lady did have an asthma attack but it was most certainly caused by an unnatural catalyst."

"Oh?" Naomi shuffled her chair marginally closer and leaned in.

"Foul play, Naomi, of the foulest sort, I'm afraid." He paused for dramatic effect before adding, "Murder."

Naomi felt the shiver which ran up her spine, her eyes wide as saucers.

The detective had a well-spoken voice, with a slight northern accent, and could almost have been reading the news headlines or narrating a Sherlock Holmes audiobook so well-controlled was his tone as he continued, "Yes, and by that most cowardly of means… Poison!"

Naomi clasped her hand over her mouth so that her sharp intake of breath wouldn't be heard by the neighbouring tables.

"Poison?" She whispered back.

"Yes, rodenticide for certain the lab thinks, though we have yet to find the means of infection. As this is now a murder case we will need to come back to the dance hall tomorrow morning to interview you all. In the meantime, I would be grateful if you could keep this information to yourself."

"Of course," Naomi's mind whirred with the news. *Rat poison?* "But she was in the car alone… other than Tony, I mean, but he seemed to be as blindsided as the rest of us. It took nine sugars to balance the effects of the shock enough so that the poor bloke could speak again."

"Quite so, which makes the whole case rather intriguing, doesn't it?" Timpson flashed another roguish smile and Naomi couldn't help but smile back.

The arrival of Sarah at Naomi's table brought a halt to the hushed conversation as Timpson downed the last of his soft drink, "I'll bid you goodnight, ladies, detective work calls."

The women said goodbye and watched the retreating form of the man, his tall frame slightly stooped, his open raincoat hanging loosely from broad shoulders.

"Do you know him?" Sarah asked, "Can't remember seeing him in here before, though he was in the café earlier today too, likes his coffee very strong as I recall."

"No, not really, our paths crossed when I was a teenager, but he always spoke with my parents. He worked with my dad's former partner."

"Oh, was your dad a detective too?"

"Yes, but he retired early to help mum with the estate. Shall we order some food?" Naomi was never keen to talk about her early life, especially with new friends whom she didn't want to burden with the heaviness of her history and the difficulty of her transition to normal family life.

"Definitely, I'll grab us a menu. I can highly recommend the chilli con carne, as Kath made it this afternoon. It's her signature dish." Sarah sat an electronic baby monitor screen on the table beside her.

"Perfect, I'll have that then," Naomi stretched her back as she took off her coat, trying to work out the cricks.

"So, how did the afternoon teas go down?" Sarah asked as she sat back down a minute later with two tall glasses of rhubarb cider for them.

"Well, they didn't get tasted at all really… Nobody had much of an appetite after the discovery of the dead body…"

"Yes! I heard about Patricia from the guy who delivers my milk for the café in the mornings. I'm not surprised that another bad thing happened up there, but it's still so sad. She was a regular in here on the weekends. Such a flirt, but fun with it, if you know what I mean? Always surrounded by a gaggle of men."

"Yes, it was certainly shocking," Naomi agreed, taking a sip of her cider. "That's lovely, not too sweet, not too tangy. So, you said you live above the pub here?"

"I do, with Rose and Kath over there, she was my Jamie's mum and she took me in when he passed."

"I'm so sorry for your loss," Naomi said, wishing she could backtrack.

"Thank you, it was very sudden. He was coming back off his first tour abroad with the army, but it wasn't active duty that got him killed. No, he was involved in a fatal car crash just south of Durham. So close to home. I was six months pregnant at the time."

"That's so awful, Sarah, I'm glad you had family here to look after you."

"Yes, I have Kath here, and Jamie's sister down in Whitley Bay. They've both been very good to me.

"At least you have Rose, so your husband lives on in her," Naomi hoped that was an okay thing to say.

"Yes, she's my silver lining around a very dark cloud

that I haven't even really begun to process yet. If it hadn't been Jamie's encouragement that prompted me to set up the coffee shop and micro bakery in the first place, I would probably have just closed the place and let the lease slide. But Jamie wouldn't have wanted that," Sarah sighed almost imperceptibly and forced a smile that didn't reach her eyes. "Anyway, tell me about you. How did you become a patisserie chef, in Bakerslea of all places?"

"Ah, well that all started in Baker's Rise with Granny Betty and Granny Hilda, both honorary grandmothers, adopted you could say…" Naomi forced down the grief, reminding herself that her new friend had much more reason to be sad, and launched into her bakery journey.

Telling the familiar story brought Naomi a sense of peace as she recalled her raison d'être. She left the pub that night with a renewed sense of purpose, determined to pull Ginger's back from the brink and make the next afternoon tea dance – still scheduled for two days' time – the best ever.

It was only when she got into bed, a feathery, green ball snoring softly on the spare pillow beside her, that Naomi went over their conversation again in her head and recalled what Sarah had said about bad things happening here in the manor house. She was sure her new friend had said something similar the other day in Three B's too.

Forcing herself not to do a Google search at this late hour, Naomi fell into a fitful, restless sleep full of unsettling dreams.

CHAPTER THIRTEEN

The best laid plans, and all that jazz, Naomi thought to herself the next day as she left Goldie's private living room, having tried and failed to persuade her boss to rally before the place was past being resurrected as a viable business concern. Goldie, lying outstretched and prone on a motheaten chaise longue had made a show of listening, though Naomi had the impression the woman was more focused on scrolling through the photos of Ginger on her phone. Despite thorough searches of the place both yesterday when the cat was noticed missing and again first thing this morning, not even a furball had been found to indicate the feline's whereabouts. It was almost as if, having succeeded in gaining her freedom, the cat simply didn't wish to be located.

"Surely, you can't afford all of your investment in this place to be wasted?" Naomi had asked, hoping that would ignite a sense of concern in the older woman.

"Who have you been speaking to? It's simply a cashflow problem," Goldie had barked back, her eyes narrowing as she tuned into the conversation fully.

"Nobody," Naomi had tried to reassure her, to build a sense of trust for their working relationship going forwards – if there was to be one at all, which didn't seem likely at this point.

"Well, you can tell Colin I'm not selling any of my jewellery, not a single pearl, do you understand? And next time tell him to do his own dirty work!"

Naomi had been shocked into silence, before deciding that trying to refute the claim she was in cahoots with the gardener, accountant, whoever he was, would be pointless anyway given the woman's mood. So, she had left Goldie as she had found her, though Naomi herself now shared the general sense of impending doom that shrouded the place.

"Naomi, my darling, how about a little vegetable frittata for Alfonso, eh?"

Naomi gave the dancer her most withering look as she hurried through the ballroom on her way back upstairs to collect Reggie. The little parrot was snoozing peacefully in his cage, and it seemed a shame to wake him, but the decision was made for her as a heavy knocking on the main doors downstairs startled the bird awake.

"Visitors! Visitors with money!" The parrot screeched, doing nothing to help Naomi's frayed nerves.

"I'll get it," Tom shouted, making his way down the main staircase.

Naomi followed, presuming that after her conversation with detective Timpson the previous evening she could accurately predict who was standing on their doorstep. She was not wrong, as she reached the bottom of the stairs just as Timpson was following Tom into the kitchen. Behind the detective was a smaller person wearing a huge black overcoat, giving the impression they were playing dress up in their father's clothing.

Naomi followed the small group into the kitchen, angry parrot on shoulder, hopping from one foot to the other and muttering complaints under his breath.

"Good morning, this is Detective Argyll, we are here to take some statements regarding what has now become a murder investigation into the death of Patricia Bonham-Smythe," Timpson spoke so formally, in such a monotone, that Naomi could tell he had delivered similar updates many times before. The man looked even more exhausted than he had the previous night, large, dark circles under-rimming his eyes, and Naomi hurried to put on the kettle to make them all some coffee.

Her movement caught the attention of the smaller detective, who suddenly noticed the parrot on Naomi's shoulder.

"Oh! What a sweet wee birdie!" The woman had a high-pitched voice in a thick Scottish brogue.

As he was wont to do, Reggie recognised immediately that a compliment was meant for him. Before Naomi could stop the eager parrot, he was back across the room and had landed on the new detective's overcoat, perching on one of the huge lapels gracefully.

"Reggie," Naomi said in a warning tone.

"Perhaps another room would be, ah, quieter," Timpson said, eying the bird.

Just as Reggie himself squawked, "You sexy beast!"

Argyll stretched a hand out from where it had been

hidden in the too-long sleeves and stroked Reggie's head, a wide grin on her face, "Bonnie birdie."

This confused Reggie, whose head shot around towards the door, looking for "My Bon-bon?"

To add to the confusion, Alfonso appeared in the kitchen at this exact point to see if the arrival had been his overdue dance tutee. Seeing the Italian and not the object of his affections, Reggie took great insult.

"Silly old trout!" He shrieked, flying at the dancer and flapping his wings in the shocked man's face.

"Reginald parrot! Perch or cage!" Naomi used her sternest voice this time.

Knowing that she meant it, the bird reluctantly retreated, though not before throwing a final insult at Alfonso.

"Mio dio!" The Italian shouted, "Excusing me! So rudes!" His English slipped in his consternation, whilst the man's first thought was to check his hair. He needn't have worried, that stiff quiff was going nowhere.

"Perhaps you'd like to begin with Mr. Di Marco, in the ballroom where it's quieter? There are plenty of tables in there for you to set up a workspace uninterrupted,"

Tom gestured to the door and Timpson gave him a nod of thanks as he and Argyll left the room.

"Not mees, I busy!" Alfonso protested, but Tom encouraged the man to follow the two detectives with an encouraging finger in the small of his back.

"Well, that was quite the scene," Naomi walked over to stand beside Reggie, stroking his soft back, "and you didn't help, mister." One rub of his head on her wrist, one softly chirped, "My No me," and of course she couldn't stay mad at the little guy for long. To be fair, the whole thing had been very confusing for all involved, especially a small bird of even smaller brain.

Carys appeared then, and more importantly, she had Bonnie with her.

"Just come to help," the Welshwoman said cheerily, though Naomi had begun to suspect that her neighbour was sure to pop up wherever there might be some juicy news to pass along to her knitting group.

"My Bon-bon!" Reggie squawked, hopping about excitedly from one foot to the other as Carys brought the grey parrot over to the wide perch that had arrived the day before.

"Give me a cwtch," Carys said, and Bonnie leaned her

head in and cuddled against her. "Give me a kiss," she leaned down to meet her cheek with the parrot's beak.

A quick learner, Reggie tried his luck too, "Give me a kiss!" Unfortunately, all Bonnie gave him was a dismissive side-eye before she took the spot on the perch farthest from her would-be suitor.

"Give her some space," Naomi encouraged him, only for Reggie to hide his face under one wing. Whether really hurt or feigning upset, Naomi wasn't sure, but the kettle had already clicked off and she had work to do.

CHAPTER FOURTEEN

"I have no ideas about any poisoning of rats!" Naomi heard Alfonso exclaim as she carried in a tray of mugs and a large French press filled with fresh coffee, "I am dance teacher!"

"You live in the caravan park, up on the headland by the medieval church, don't you?" Timpson asked.

"Yes," the Italian's eyes narrowed, and his tone was one of suspicion.

"And are you up to date on your rent payments?"

"I don't see how that's any of interests," the Italian was getting angry now, his hand fisted on the table. When he saw Naomi's gaze fixed on it, he quickly hid his arm under the fuchsia tablecloth.

"Well, I have it on good authority that you have been given your final notice and must surely be looking for another place to stay. I would warrant that you must be hoping one of your dance students – all women of rather advanced age, I might add – would take you in. What exact services are you offering, Mr. Di Marco? And how much do you charge for them? I'm sure some husbands in town would be very angry if their wives told them. Enough for you to have shut one of those wives up if she threatened to do so, perhaps. Just conjecture, of course."

Wow, Timpson was good! But then he had learnt from the best, Naomi thought, wishing she could be a fly on the wall for the rest of the interview. She took one last look at Alfonso, who was now puce in the face to match today's garish, satin top. He looked like he was either about to explode in venomous rebuttal of the accusations, or bend over and be sick. Clearly, his body hadn't yet decided and the Italian simply sat stone still, his eyes wide and glassy, his mouth open like a shocked goldfish.

Timpson, in stark contrast, barely paused for breath, "The late woman's husband has reported her having a few nosebleeds this week and suffering from out of character headaches and confusion. She had called him her ex-husband's name a few times. Did she mention any of that to you? Did you notice any decline in her health during your time together? More breathless whilst dancing, or whilst doing other activities, perhaps..? I assume you knew she was asthmatic."

Naomi had learned from her dad never to repeat official conversations, but as she returned to the kitchen she could tell the rumour mill had got there before her.

"Now, you know I'm not one to gossip," Carys was saying, her Welsh accent always becoming more pronounced when she was, in fact, about to gossip, "but I've heard from Deirdre who cleans the caravans, that Alfonso barely sleeps in his own bed. Always gallivanting. And it doesn't take much to guess where he's laying his head, does it? Not with the way our Goldie lavishes attention on him. Mind you, so do all his other women."

Tom flashed Naomi a look of 'thank goodness your back' and immediately excused himself to go and transfer the photos from the opening day to the detectives.

"Well, it's probably best to not speculate, given it's a murder enquiry," Naomi said.

"Hmph, well, I can feel it in my bones he's a badun!" Carys declared, before stomping off and leaving Naomi with both parrots. The pair seemed to have shuffled closer in their sleep, both with their heads hidden under their wings, and Naomi snapped a quick photo on her phone to send to Flora and Adam.

An hour later it was Naomi herself in the hot seat, feeling she was more in a strange dream than at a police interview, what with the drooping hot pink and silver balloons left over from the aborted grand opening, and Classic FM playing what sounded like a funeral dirge in the background. The room was hot and smelled foisty, as if there was damp and mould in the corners which had simply been painted over and not treated. Naomi wouldn't be surprised if Goldie had cut all the corners just to get the place open. The whole room could do with a good airing, the heavy velvet curtains clearly trapping the mustiness inside.

Timpson too, was obviously not unaffected by the conditions, the man loosening his tie slightly before deciding that small difference would not have enough effect and jumping to his feet.

"Excuse me for a moment, Naomi," he said, rushing to the elevated dance stage and turning off the radio, then opening all the curtains on their side of the room before sitting back down. The original, wooden windows were not double glazed, and the patches where they were rotting let in a considerable draught. Thankfully, the fresh air soon reached the trio and the detective began again. They talked briefly about how long Naomi had been at Ginger's, her role there, and what she had seen on the day of the deceased's demise. It wasn't a long conversation, as those answers could be easily given as 'just a week, flexible, and very little.'

"And what do you think of your new colleagues?" Timpson asked, one eyebrow raised slightly.

"Well, er..." Naomi was unsure how to proceed. She had been trying, after a lot of therapy in her late teens, to not project her own feelings of lack of self-worth onto others, particularly by being too judgy. She was still very much a work in progress in that regard, she knew, but speaking badly about people she'd only just met didn't sit well with her.

"I would remind you you're on tape and what you say will be kept confidential," Argyll spoke for the first time since Naomi had entered the room. Mainly, the petite detective had spent the time since the curtains were opened looking at the birds in the gardens outside. The heavy coat remained, and Naomi wondered briefly how the woman hadn't melted in it.

"Yes, of course," Naomi began, still hesitant, "well, Tom is lovely, seems very level headed, works with your department so I guess you know that already, um, Carys has a parrot, loves knitting and er, has a keen interest in the lives of her neighbours," Naomi caught the small smile which Timpson quickly contained, "then there's Alfonso, whom you've seen for yourselves, I don't think I can add anything there, and Colin who has, um, a sweet spot for Goldie and a realistic idea of the finances here."

"Very good," Timpson smiled fully now, small lines appearing at the sides of his eyes before the expression was gone as quickly as it had come as he asked his next question. "And Harriet Hornsley, er Goldie as she is known?"

"Well, er dramatic certainly, cat lover, keen amateur dancer, quite flaky when it comes to facts and figures, such as defining my role and repaying me for goods bought," Naomi tried and failed to not sound bitter. "Devastated by the events of this week, I think, has lost all motivation to continue with the dance hall. Um, is that enough?"

Timpson ignored Naomi's question and instead asked, "And what about Harriet's relationship with Alfonso, do you believe it to be… more intimate than simple dance tutor and student, or employer and employee."

"I think Goldie would like it to be, but I have no knowledge of whether it is," Naomi said honestly.

"And has she mentioned her friendship with the deceased either directly to you or in your presence?"

"Not really, I only know that they've known each other socially for years and there may have been some, er, well, sharing of husbands… no, not in the way that sounds!" Naomi realised what she had said and felt the hot blush creep up her neck. "I just mean, they moved in the same social circles and knew the same men. I really have no evidence of this, so probably not the best to ask, I'm afraid."

"Not at all, you've done extremely well, than…" Timpson's thanks was interrupted as Goldie appeared from the doorway that led to her rooms. How long she had been standing there in the shadows, Naomi didn't know, but she hoped the woman hadn't heard anything of what she'd just said.

"Ah, Mrs. Hornsley, perfect timing," Detective Argyll said, whilst Naomi caught Timpson's eye and he gave her a kind smile, no doubt to try to alleviate the awkward atmosphere.

"Where is my lunch, girl?" Goldie asked Naomi, deliberately ignoring the police presence.

"I'll ask Carys," Naomi said, standing hurriedly and wanting to get as far away from the woman as possible. She bit her tongue on her other possible retorts, said goodbye to the detectives and hurried from the room and straight to the large double doors in the entrance hall.

Unfortunately, no amount of gulping in fresh air could rid her of the unsettled feeling, the suffocating anxiety that this old house had filled her with right now, and so Naomi rushed back to grab Reggie from the kitchen where he now snoozed alone, grabbed his carrier from her room, and set off into town with no exact destination in mind.

CHAPTER FIFTEEN

Naomi's frantic feet brought her to the Three B's café, and she paused only a moment on the doorstep before going inside the cheery coffee shop. Hit by an immediate smell of baking bread mixed with one of her favourite scents of all, freshly ground coffee, Naomi breathed in deeply as she deposited the small bird carrier onto the nearest chair. No doubt sensing her mood, or maybe just lulled back to sleep by the quick pace of her walking, Reggie had been uncharacteristically quiet the whole way here.

"Naomi! How are you?" Sarah came from behind the counter to give her a quick hug, careful of the sleeping baby strapped to her front.

"A bit frazzled, to be honest," Naomi forced a smile.

"Then let me get you some coffee and a slice of banana bread, just out of the oven."

Naomi noticed the paper-wrapped packages lined up on the counter, "Sounds perfect. Do you get a lot of daily orders?"

"Yes, I have my regulars for sourdough loaves and then there's the sweet tooth brigade as I like to call them, who make frequent requests for the chocolate cakes and brownies. Today, I had several orders for banana loaves too, so I made extra for the coffee shop."

"Sounds like heaven… Regular customers, working in your own space… Maybe I've made all the wrong choices," Naomi kept her tone light, but for the first time in a long while it seriously crossed her mind to use some of the money in the account her parents had set up for her. *Surely a little business like this would be easier than working for French men with wandering hands and a God complex or demanding women with a fragile grasp on reality. But then, couldn't I just have stayed at the Tearoom on the Rise if I didn't want anything more than a cosy coffee shop?*

Naomi's musings were cut short by a few loud squawks from the bird carrier. Always annoyed to be in that confined space, but even more so when he'd woken suddenly, believed he'd been placed in there stealthily and to top it all off was being ignored, Reggie made his feelings clear.

"Oh! Who's that?" Sarah asked, just noticing the carrier. Peering through the soft, meshed, see through front she spotted Reggie, who clamped his beak shut and tilted his head to the side to study Sarah in return.

"That's my parrot, well, my family's parrot. Reggie's staying with me for a while, just to add more chaos to my first week," Naomi unzipped the travel case. "Is it okay if he hops onto my shoulder? I won't let him fly around?"

"Of course, what a cutie!"

Reggie hopped straight out, though remained remarkably quiet, studying the small person on Sarah's front.

"That's my baby, Rose," Sarah said, moving the fabric next to the baby's head to give the parrot a better view.

"Bay-bie bird!" Reggie squawked, enamoured by the tiny, raven-haired child, "Best bay-bie!"

"Aw that's so sweet," Sarah bent closer.

"Don't be fooled, he can be a bit of a character when he wants," Naomi said, just as the bell over the door chimed and a familiar detective bent to get under the low frame.

Sarah stood up to welcome the customer just as Reggie proved Naomi's warning correct.

"Not that jerk!" He shrieked at Timpson.

"Reggie!" Naomi tapped the bird's beak, "I'm so sorry, Detective, Reggie's previous owner, the one before Flora, taught him some, er, rather colourful phrases."

"I remember," the detective said, "double macchiato to go please and some of that lovely looking banana bread. Thanks."

Sarah returned behind the counter to prepare the coffees whilst Timpson perched on the chair nearest the door, which happened to be at Naomi's table.

"Tough morning?" Naomi asked gently, watching the man scrub his hands over his face.

"Tough couple of years," Timpson replied, before quickly catching himself. "Sorry, yes, that ballroom has given me quite the headache."

"And strong coffee is the answer?" Naomi teased him

gently.

"Ha, well, it'll give me the kick I need to get through the afternoon," he smiled wryly.

"Do you think the investigation will be a long one?" Naomi asked, knowing she was veering on territory their discussion shouldn't enter.

"Um, no, I doubt it. We've got Motive, we know the Method, just need the Means. The effects of the poison seem to have gradually built up over days, so I need to work out how that was administered. Once I get that, I reckon everything will be tied up pretty quickly. The Means should point to the murderer, or at least confirm our suspicions."

"Wow, that is quick," Naomi said.

"Small town like this, limited suspects, not so difficult," Timpson said matter-of-factly.

"Do you live near here?" Naomi really had no idea why she'd asked that.

The man's eyebrows raised slightly, but he answered in the same even tone he had with her other questions, "Not far, just up the coast in Alnmouth. I get sent all around this side of Northumberland, all the way up to Berwick, there's not so much serious crime in

Northumberland to have me centred in one place. We have a station just down the road though, so that's handy as a base when I'm in this area."

Naomi wanted to ask the man more about his life since Baker's Rise but she already felt like she was prying, so she was relieved when Sarah brought the man's coffee over in a takeaway cup with a paper bag containing his slice of loaf cake.

"I'll bid you ladies good day," Timpson said, rather old-fashionedly, ducking out of the door and disappearing across the town square.

"He seems like a lovely man, been in about five times in the past couple of days, I probably shouldn't be encouraging his coffee habit," Sarah laughed, the gentle movement waking the baby who was already stirring.

"Oh, Rosie Roo, there she is," Sarah cooed at the infant, unclipping the baby carrier and freeing her squirming legs.

"Rosie-Roo" Reggie parroted back, "Bay-bee bird. Best Bay-bee Rosie-Roo!"

"Aw, he can be so sweet," Sarah said to Naomi.

"He has his moments," Naomi agreed, cuddling

Reggie in the crook of her neck.

"If you could just grab her, I'll get our drinks and cake. The coffees are already made," Sarah said, handing Naomi the baby before Naomi could form a response.

"Oh! Okay," she took the little girl, currently soothed by sucking on her dummy, and was immediately worried that she didn't know how to hold her correctly.

"You've got her fine, don't worry," Sarah said, sensing Naomi's nerves before she turned back to the counter.

"You stay up there, Reggie," Naomi said, though the bird hadn't ventured from her shoulder, so mesmerized was he by the little human. "You've seen babies before," Naomi told him.

"It might be the hair," Sarah said, "she does have an exceptional amount of it, did right when she was born, and it's so thick. Look, she almost has a little fringe!"

It was true and as Naomi studied the babe in her arms, as she drank in that distinctive smell and watched Rose's tiny hand grasp her finger, she wondered why she'd always avoided contact with children. Her own history, of course, was the explanation, but right now Naomi wondered why she continued to let her past dictate her future. Why she couldn't just break free of it all and, well, live the life she was meant to have.

Avoiding connection, avoiding intimacy, she was denying herself the right to be a mother and to have a family of her own, and Naomi had to ask herself,

Is that really what I want?

CHAPTER SIXTEEN

Naomi had just got into her fluffy pyjamas and settled Reggie on his pillow for the night, the soft light from the bedside lamp making the little parrot's feathers shine a deep jade, when a quiet knock on the bedroom door drew her attention.

"There's somebody at the door," Reggie chirped sleepily, stating the obvious, though he clearly didn't think the gentle noise warranted him actually moving from his cosy spot.

"You wait there then, I'll get it," Naomi cocked an eyebrow at the little bird before shuffling across the threadbare carpet in her thick bed socks.

The moment the bedroom door was opened wide enough for him to fit through, Tom squeezed in, an open laptop in his hands and a furtive look about him.

"Sorry to barge in, but I wanted to show you this," he said, moving straight to the small desk by the window.

Not known for her neatness, Naomi still had to put away her few possessions, so she quickly cleared a space for the laptop and gestured for Tom to take the battered velvet swivel chair.

"So, I was just deleting these photos from my cloud, which I always do when they've been uploaded at the other end by the in-house forensics team, and I spotted this," Tom looked up for the first time and clocked that Naomi was in her nightwear. "Oh! You were about to go to bed!"

"Well, it is quarter past midnight."

"Sorry, I was on the late shift today, just got back. Do you mind if I show you quickly?" He was like an excited boy, his eyes shining brightly and his hair all fluffy from where he'd been raking his fingers through it as he worked. How could she say no?

"Of course, go ahead, I'm guessing it's something from

the opening day?"

"It is. So, you see here, this picture of the limo door opening, then this next one I caught the body before Tony got into the frame in the next photo. So, this middle one, you can clearly see the blood under her nose and on her lips, which is what I'd previously focused on. Tonight, for some reason, though, I scanned the whole image and spotted this," he used the mousepad to zoom in, not on the woman but on the footwell in front of the deceased's feet.

"I'm, um, not sure I can see anyth…" Naomi began.

"Wait for it, there's only a tiny bit visible," Tom's excitement was contagious as he zoomed in even further.

Naomi leaned forward to get a better look, and sure enough when Tom sat back to give her a clearer view she spotted it too. "What is that?"

"Well, I can't be certain, but given the round edge, the thin gold rim and the flash of blue enamel that's visible, I'd say it's maybe a piece of jewellery?"

"Or a case of some sort? Like a medication case?" Naomi suggested.

"Could be, either way it must've been kicked under the

driver's seat when the body was being checked by Tony, Goldie, and then me. If you look on this final pic I took before the police arrived, once I knew there was no pulse and I wanted to document the exact position of the body as we found it, the mysterious item is no longer visible."

"Now, that is interesting," Naomi's curiosity was piqued, and she suddenly felt a lot less tired than she had ten minutes ago. "Do you think the police know about it."

"If they don't now, then they will shortly. Either the team will pick it up on the photos like I have or the forensics guys focusing on the interior of the car will do. Contrary to those mystery books that make the police look dim-witted, we're actually quite a clever bunch!" He smiled to soften the words.

"I realise that," Naomi became indignant, "my dad is the smartest person I know!"

"Sorry, sorry," he rubbed her shoulder as an apology for teasing her.

Naomi, who normally avoided physical contact, flinched noticeably, straightening suddenly as Tom quickly pulled his hand away.

"It's okay," Naomi whispered to fill the uncomfortable moment.

"So, er, you never did tell me why you came here, of all places?" Tom spoke at the same time, as keen as she was to change the subject, and they both gave a small laugh.

Naomi sat on the edge of the bed as Tom swivelled the desk chair to face her, "Well, for a couple of years I'd felt I needed to get out of my comfort zone. I was running my mum's tearoom in Baker's Rise and doing a bit of external catering on the side, but although everyone praised my baking skills, I felt I was lacking in formal training, if you know what I mean? Some kind of professional validation. So, I found an ad online for a hotel in Paris which was looking for a trainee patisserie chef and I took it."

"That's impressive, do you speak French?" Tom asked.

"Nope, hadn't even visited the country on holiday before. Really liked the film 'Ratatouille,' so saw that as a good sign and just went for it. Never been so impulsive in my life, and in hindsight there's a reason I was always so cautious."

"It didn't go well?" Tom wheeled the chair forward slightly, his eyes fixed on hers.

"Disaster from start to finish," Naomi whispered. "Not only did the other chefs treat me with derision because it was immediately clear I didn't know the proper way to do anything, as well as not speaking their precious language of course, but the head patisserie chef took, ah, a particular interest in me from my very first day."

"Oh?" Tom looked concerned.

"Yes, it started with him making jokes about my lack of understanding, then standing too close for comfort as he was demonstrating the baking methods, making gross comments about my appearance and his open marriage, and that was just for starters… and ended with me slapping him across the face when he squeezed my bottom and tried to kiss me one evening when we were both clearing up together. All the others had gone home, and I guess he just saw his chance."

"My goodness, Naomi, did you report him for sexual harassment?"

"The hotel owner preferred to keep her experienced chef over a naïve English girl, so she disregarded my many complaints."

"Many? How long were you there for?"

"Just under six months. I know I should've left sooner,

but... pride, it's such an unfaithful companion. Makes you want to stick things out to prove yourself right and others wrong even when the real decision is glaringly obvious."

"Well, if it's any consolation, you're not the only person to have tried to forge your own path, only to realise you should've listened to those who spoke words of caution," Tom shook his head self-deprecatingly.

"You don't think I was stupid?" Naomi asked, her voice barely audible above the snores of the parrot behind her.

"No, it's hard to get out of situations once we're in them," he replied cryptically.

"It really is," she agreed, "so hard to make the decision to go back with our tail between our legs. And that's how I ended up here. Not wanting to return to Baker's Rise under the cloud of shame of my first failed venture out of the village."

"Would your parents and friends not have been supportive?" Tom asked.

"Oh no, they would absolutely have welcomed me back with love and open arms, it was my own self view that made me take the first baking job in Northumberland that I could find. Had my wings well and truly clipped, so although I didn't want to go home, I still wanted to be close."

"That makes sense," Tom's smile was gentle as he stood, "anyway, I've kept you up late enough. Good to chat to you, Naomi, glad to get to know you better."

His gaze was so earnest, so compelling, that Naomi had to drag her eyes away from his face.

"See you in the morning," she said, holding the door halfway open.

"Goodnight Naomi."

CHAPTER SEVENTEEN

The next day began early with a loud commotion downstairs, startling both Naomi and Reggie awake.

"Get out of it! Shut yer face!" The little bird shrieked, covering his own face with a wing and snuggling back into his pillow.

"Wait here," Naomi told him, grabbing a hoody from the pile on her backpack and pulling it over her head, "goodness knows what's happening now."

She followed an equally bleary-eyed Carys down the stairs, though the older woman was at least dressed. "Is Tom not home? He can't have slept through that surely?" Naomi asked her neighbour, looking to see if the man in question was following them down.

"Left for work first thing," the Welshwoman said.

"More first thing than this?" Naomi grumbled, wondering how the man managed to function on so little sleep.

As it turned out, it was nine o'clock in the morning and Naomi had slept through her alarm. They reached the entrance hall to be faced with Goldie's high-pitched shrieks and Colin fawning around her like a long-suffering courtier.

Without any caffeine in her, Naomi was ill-prepared for the dramatic outburst and snapped out a curt, "Calm down!"

Unused to being spoken to in such a manner, the shock from those words had the effect of silencing Goldie enough for Colin to get a word in edgewise.

"Cat poo," he said, looking very pleased with himself, "in the corridor here." He pointed to the narrow, dark hallway which Naomi had as yet had no cause to venture into.

Goldie was not one to be silenced for long, however, pulling the tie on her semi-sheer nightdress and matching robe tighter around her waist and quickly finding her voice, "Well go on then man! You've woken me up and dragged me out here waffling on about my Ginger, I assumed you'd found her. Get a move on, and we'll all search along there. I'm sure you could've located her without my help, now you're onto a trail of clues…" The woman continued to mutter as the four of them started along the dank corridor in a line, Colin first, then Goldie, Carys and lastly Naomi.

It felt almost farcical, like one of those Scooby Doo cartoons she used to watch as a child, and had the whole corridor not reeked of both cat faeces and mould, Naomi wouldn't have been so keen to rush forward towards the old conservatory with them all.

"I was just coming to my office, first time in a few days," Colin explained, pointing to the first door they passed on the right with a dirty, soil-covered hand, "and I spotted it. Mind where you step there…"

The warning came too late for poor Carys, who had already stepped one squishy slipper into the mess left by the infamous Ginger. There was no time to deal with that now though, as Goldie grabbed the housekeepers elbow and urged her forward, past two more closed doors and finally, thankfully, into the light and fresh air of the windowed room.

"Did we look in here before?" Goldie barked.

There was a general, mumbling consensus of 'no,' to which the woman became momentarily enraged, before obviously remembering she needed their help and plastering on one of her usual theatrical smiles. "Let's get to work then, my dears."

It took barely any time at all, before a fluffy orange tail was spotted beneath one of the dust-filled, rattan chairs that sat against the far wall.

"Ginger Pawgers! Mummy's baby!" Goldie cooed as Naomi, being by far the youngest and most agile, was tasked with encouraging the hissing cat out of her cosy corner.

When diplomacy and bribery failed, physical action had to be taken, to the detriment of Naomi's poor hands which ended up sliced by the angry feline's claws. Thankful for her long sleeves, Naomi went back in for a final time, hands covered with a random, very dusty sheet that must've been covering the chair and been knocked off by the cat as she sought a place to hide. Success was hers, much to the anger of the animal, which hissed and spat at Goldie, even going so far as to scratch her owner across the face as Naomi tried to hand over the scrabbling creature.

"Why you..!" Goldie began, lifting a menacing hand, before remembering her audience, "You must be so scared my little one."

"What's this?" Naomi, still on her knees, leant forward and grabbed the shiny white tin that had been hidden behind the oversized pet, pulling it out from under the chair and into the light.

"I wouldn't be touching that, if I were you," Colin said ominously, "it has a warning label on this side."

The manky sheet once again came to her aid as Naomi turned the small tin to read the label.

'For the swift and humane elimination of rodents...'

"It's rat poison!" Carys screeched, her whiffy slippers forgotten in light of the adrenaline-fuelling discovery.

"It can't be," Goldie said dismissively, halfway to the door, the struggling cat wrapped firmly in her chiffon robe and currently slicing holes through the thin material.

"It only blummin' well is!" Colin confirmed, grabbing the tin from the floor with no thought to either fingerprints or poisonous substance.

"Bring it back to the kitchen, it's freezing in here," the

leader barked the order so Colin obeyed, hurrying back through to the kitchen with the toxic pot clutched to his chest like a prize.

"You're telling me you moved it? And with your bare hands?" Detective Timpson's voice was the least controlled Naomi had ever heard it, as she clicked on the kettle half an hour later, and settled back against the counter to watch the show.

"It was mine to move. In my property, I mean," Goldie stuttered. Thankfully the cat had already been deposited in the woman's own rooms and Naomi doubted her boss would be back in here now if she hadn't been summoned by the detective.

"And covered in… What is that? Soil? Not to mention possible fingerprints smudged and overwritten. What do you have to say about it, Mr. Chillingham? Shall I bring you in for tampering with evidence?"

"What? No, I was just acting under orders. And it was pure coincidence I've been up and gardening already," he quickly threw Goldie under the bus to save his own skin, and it didn't go unnoticed by the woman who now glared in the gardener's direction.

"If Thomas were here he would have explained how we should keep the crime scene, ah…" Goldie searched for the right word.

"Intact," Timpson ground out. "Only a fool would not realise the tin should've been left, untouched where it was found," his voice was lower now, but strangely enough not calmer. More like the detective's fury had been hastily contained within his chest and only allowed to release through those low, staccato sentences. If Naomi did not already know him to be a reasonable, professional man, she would have been afraid. "Mrs. Hornsley, I can honestly say you couldn't have messed this up more if you'd tried."

At that criticism, Goldie launched into a dramatic, messy sobbing episode, shunning Colin's attempts to calm her and Carys' offers of tea and toast.

"Oh, really! This is quite the performance," Timpson flashed the woman one final, disgusted look, before turning his attention to Naomi, who so far had been a silent bystander to the whole discussion. The tin of rat poison was currently being roughly shoved into a plastic evidence bag by Argyll, who had also chosen the path of least attention, and had so far been loitering out in the hallway. Wearing a pair of thick, protective gloves, at least three sizes bigger than her hands, it took the detective four attempts to pick up the slippery tin and had the situation not been so serious, Naomi might have found it comical.

All the while, Naomi could see Timpson's rage growing. It was not overtly noticeable, but there were subtle signs behind the man's staring, slightly twitching eyes, for example, and in his tightly clenched jaw.

When they locked gazes, though, the detective's expression softened slightly, "Naomi, when things around here have, ah, calmed down, please could you have a check around for anything else… out of the ordinary. I'll get forensics into the conservatory and anywhere else you suggest they look. Oh, and if you see Mr. Di Marco, please let him know I'd like to see him at the station… pronto."

"Will do," Naomi nodded, silently wishing she could leave with the two detectives who were beating a hasty retreat from the bedlam currently surrounding them.

CHAPTER EIGHTEEN

As could have been easily predicted, Goldie had retired to her rooms then, after making her disappointment with them all clear, and laying the blame for everything firmly at Colin's door. Enraged, the man had stormed out of the kitchen, vowing to "leave the sinking ship to drown, with Goldie being the fattest rat on it." Their boss had played down the man's threatening insult, but had been visibly shaken, feigning a fainting episode and requiring Carys to help her back to her quarters. There had been no sign at all of Alfonso, so Naomi assumed the dancer had received the detective's message to head down to the station.

With everyone therefore either occupied or no longer

in the building, Naomi decided to give herself the day off and headed back to bed with a mug of coffee and a packet of chocolate digestives. The bedroom was freezing, so she added a woolly hat and a scarf to her mismatching attire and snuggled under the covers. A hot shower was out of the question, since Naomi had learned the hard way that the water was only heated for an hour in the morning and two hours in the evening. She dreaded to imagine the age of the boiler, though judging by the clattering and clanking noises when the water was running, it was at least as old as she was.

An unexpectedly free day and time to do a bit of research was perhaps the worst thing she could have had, however, as Naomi found herself engrossed in reading about the manor house's history. Her inquisitive nature having been ignited by Sarah's random references to the old place, Naomi skimmed through every newspaper article and reference she could find online, some dating back several decades. It would seem that the place's history was besmirched by intrigue and mystery, even culminating in the deaths of two of its former residents. Whether by sheer bad luck, or something more sinister, the place had earned the title 'Murder Manor' in the local area.

Now Naomi didn't really believe in hauntings or bad

juju or whatever, and having lived happily in what had been described as Baker's Rise's own 'Murder Mansion', the village itself having been dubbed by the press as a 'Murder Magnet,' Naomi didn't really care for such labels. In her experience, they were mostly used as clickbait by the press and for local gossip fodder. Nevertheless, the list of unfortunate events at her current location was indeed lengthy and rather off putting, and after a few hours of solitary scrolling Naomi took Reggie into the kitchen for a change of scenery and to find a more wholesome headspace.

"Ah, there you are lovey. Feeling okay?" Carys asked, eying Naomi's pyjama bottoms and bed socks.

"Yes, just having a day off. Goldie never did give me my work schedule," Naomi shrugged her shoulders as if that mattered little now, in light of recent events, and helped herself to some tea from the pot on the table. Covered in a hand-knitted tea cosy it reminded her suddenly of home.

"How are you doing, Carys?" Naomi asked gently, noticing the grey pallor to the older woman's normally rosy cheeks.

"My Bon-bon," Reggie squawked desolately, having done two turns flying about the room and come up empty-winged.

"Aw she's in her cage in my room, sweetheart, having an afternoon nap," Carys stroked Reggie gently on the head and he settled in her lap on top of a chunky ball of wool. Knitting needles and what appeared to be a half-knitted bobble hat sat on the table in front of them.

"I'm fine, thank you," she replied to Naomi, a stock response that slipped easily off the tongue.

"It is very unsettling and upsetting to be at the centre of a police investigation, it'd be very understandable to be feeling a bit shaken," Naomi ventured, "I certainly am."

"Well, now you come to mention it petal, I am feeling a bit out of sorts. Goldie's usual demands are bad enough, but her temper today, well…"

"You know you don't have to put up with it, don't you? You could walk away. She doesn't own you," Naomi knew immediately that she'd said too much when the Welshwoman stood abruptly, sending Reggie into flight once again.

"Look at those scratches. That cat is wild, I tell you. Let me get the Savlon cream out of the cupboard."

"Oh! Thank you," Naomi encouraged Reggie onto her shoulder, wondering how to proceed with the conversation.

"And I've got a shepherd's pie in the oven," Carys smothered the antiseptic cream liberally over the stinging lacerations on Naomi's hands, "we don't want you getting an infection in those, they're nasty."

"Thank you, Carys, that feels better. But you really don't need to feed us all, you know? Does Goldie pay you for that?"

"She doesn't pay me at all, lovey, just in room and board, so no, I can't just leave. Got nothing in my purse, have I? Can't leave my little Bonnie homeless." The woman's voice cracked on those last words and Naomi's heart went out to her. She silently vowed to have it out with Goldie on behalf of them all.

"Is that why you moved from Morpeth with her?" Naomi asked softly, grateful that for once Reggie had the sense to keep his beak shut.

"Partly, and also because of our shared history. She's the only friend I have left," Carys admitted, the loneliness echoing through her words.

"But she must pay you a proper salary, with a proper written contract, Carys, otherwise she's taking advantage of your good nature. Pure and simple. You should talk to her about it. Put your foot down."

"What? And be out on my ear with just a parrot for a pillow?" The woman sounded bitter now, though the wetness which she blinked out of her eyes belied her harsh tone.

"I could come with you to talk to her, we could explain it was on behalf of all of us employees so that you wouldn't be singled out," Naomi suggested.

"Absolutely not, and you mustn't either, do you hear me? Goldie is… well, she has a nasty streak, and you don't want to get on the wrong side of her."

Rather ominous, Naomi thought.

She let the subject drop and brought up their shared love of parrots instead as a safe topic of conversation, all the while secretly planning when she would confront their employer. The Bramble-Millers were big fans of justice, and Naomi vowed to do her family proud.

CHAPTER NINETEEN

The day dragged on, with Naomi eventually getting changed into proper clothes and venturing downstairs to do what soothed her heart most – baking. Using up the last of her ingredients from the other day, she made a batch of plain scones and an apple pie, listening to her favourite true crime podcast through her wireless earbuds as she worked – probably not sensible given recent events, but it was part of her usual routine so Naomi didn't think twice. It was as she was bending to take the pie out of the oven, that a person came up behind her and gave her the shock of her life.

"Argh!" Naomi shrieked, almost dropping the heavy

pie tin.

"It's me! Tom! Sorry, I did say your name three times as I walked across the room," he looked genuinely apologetic.

"Way to give a woman a heart attack," she jabbed him lightly in the ribs and stepped back, "shift okay?"

"Bit of a stressful day but thankfully no major crimes to attend. All quiet here?"

"I wish…" Naomi began sarcastically, before launching into a description of the morning's events.

"You're kidding! The rat poison was here? Well, that makes us all suspects."

"I hadn't thought of it like that, but yes, I guess it does," Naomi washed her hands and put on the kettle, both on automatic pilot.

"Have you been out at all? For some fresh air?" Tom asked, looking at Naomi with a concerned expression.

"Um, well, no, but I did manage to get dressed."

The man frowned, his eyes locking on hers, "Naomi, it's not healthy to be in this strained… this strange atmosphere all day. Believe me, you need to get out or it'll drive you mad. You'll start coming up with all kinds of random scenarios and ideas. Why don't we have a cuppa and some of whatever delicious fruity thing you've just created, then go for a walk along the beach. The tide's out. Have you been down there since you arrived?"

"Er, no, actually. I kept meaning to but… events."

"Well, we'll get wrapped up and go for a walk." He made the decision for them, and Naomi was happy to have someone else to do the thinking for once.

Half an hour later they left the building by a patio door hidden behind one of the heavy curtains in the ballroom. Naomi was sure she didn't know even half the rooms and entryways in the old house yet, as she followed Tom out.

"Won't this just lead to the back garden?" She asked, confused.

"Wait and see," he told her, flashing a smile back in Naomi's direction.

With Reggie settled upstairs with Carys and Bonnie, a situation which pleased the little parrot greatly, to the point that he didn't even notice her leaving, Naomi drank in the fresh air and tried to force her body to relax. She followed Tom along a gravel path which edged the floral borders of the huge lawn, admiring the last of the roses still in bloom. The mixture of their lingering scent with the salt from the nearby North Sea was not an unpleasant concoction, and Naomi tried to clear her mind of everything but her current sensory input. This proved difficult, however, when Tom seemed to be leading them to the darkest, farthest corner of the garden, and suddenly Naomi's anxiety struck up a heavy beat in her chest.

"Tom, where are we…" Naomi began, just as the man disappeared between two high privet hedges. Unsure, but trusting him still, Naomi followed to find an open wooden gate, and the man in question standing just the other side of it.

"See," Tom said, clearly pleased with himself, "we walk down this path here and then we're on the promenade. From there, just down the steps and we're onto the beach. Short cut!"

The path ahead was both narrow and steep, with overgrown foliage snaking across to form a criss-crossing ceiling of sorts. Naomi turned and shut the gate behind her, "Should we not lock this?"

"Never seems to be locked," Tom shrugged his shoulders.

"Surely that's not very safe? Anyone could come up from the promenade and get in, especially with that patio door that wasn't locked either," Naomi was quite shocked by the lackadaisical nature of her new home's security. Her dad would have something to say about it if he knew, that's for sure. She made a mental note to mention the situation to Colin, if he was still around after today's outburst that is.

With the sun low in the sky as sunset neared, the sounds of children letting off steam on the beach before bedtime, and the slight breeze which ruffled her hair, Naomi felt more alive than she had since arriving in Bakerslea. They only needed to walk a hundred metres or so along the promenade before they came to an old set of concrete steps leading directly onto the beach. Up to their left was the headland with the glass-walled Maritime Centre standing proud, and to their right a larger expanse of sand, halfway along which Naomi knew there would be steps back onto the promenade and from there to the town square where Sarah's café was situated. Happy that she was beginning to get her bearings in her new home, it was only after walking for a couple of minutes along the sand that Naomi noticed Tom was unusually quiet.

"Penny for them," she said gently.

"Huh? Oh, just thinking. Been a bit of a day and being out in nature helps me get my thoughts in order," he explained. "Sorry, I'm not being very good company."

"Not at all, and I know what you mean, it's hard to think straight when you're cooped up inside or having demands put on you at work. If there's anything I can help with, I'm more than happy to listen, or we can just walk. I'm good with either," Naomi smiled.

Tom was silent for a moment and Naomi focused on the sound of the waves away to her right, and the seagulls making their presence known overhead. At length her companion sighed deeply and began speaking in a low, hushed voice.

"My father phoned me in my lunch break today to tell me the contestation of my grandad's will has been denied. All those months going back and forth, and it didn't even get to court."

"Oh that's not good, did his solicitor give a reason?" Naomi asked.

"Just that each beneficiary had received a solid inheritance, split per my Grandad's wishes, so there was nothing to argue over. My dad got the house he had grown up in, you see, which Grandad was still living in – with Goldie of course – when he died. His brother, my uncle, got the holiday cottage in the Lake District, and the widow, Goldie, got the old manor place that Grandad had intended to be a retirement investment. He was asset rich and cash poor, you see, so all three beneficiaries got a building and not much else. My dad and his brother shared out what was left in Grandad's home after Goldie had ferreted away whatever she wanted of it while he was still alive. Horrible woman."

"So there's no point in appealing?" Naomi asked gently, aware the man beside her was getting increasingly riled as the conversation progressed.

"Dad doesn't think so. He says I should let it go now, but how can I? When that woman is still living it up? Grandad was fine when he married her, fit and well, then three months later he was gone. How does that happen?"

"Did they do a post mortem?"

"Nope, cut and dried case of myocardial infarction apparently," Tom kicked some sand up with the toe of his boot.

"Had he had any previous heart attacks?"

"A small one, a decade before, Dad says. Anyway, he

said at lunchtime that he wants me to come home, that I should just let it go as there's no proof of foul play and it's taken up enough of our lives already."

"He might be right. Can you live anywhere in the area and still get to work easily?" Naomi hoped to gently steer the topic of conversation away from the one that so clearly ate away at the man's happiness every day. It really couldn't be good for his state of mind.

"Hmm? Oh, yes, I'm more or less freelance, just a floating bloke with a camera going where I'm told to. Currently, they've given me a desk in the station down the road, but when I lived with Dad I worked from home. I know I could just pack up and go back, but what with this new murder, it's got me thinking again…"

"You think Goldie did it?" Despite knowing the man's views on the woman, Naomi was still shocked.

"Wouldn't put it past her," Tom said, "I mean, I'm pretty sure she's got form for it, just need her to trip up and give me the proof I need. And quickly. I'm well aware I chose to take her up on her conciliatory offer of free accommodation, that I willingly walked into the dragon's lair, but now I'm wondering if she'll self-combust before I can get the justice I need for my family. Anyway, sorry for burdening you with all this.

What I was actually hoping to ask was if you'd like to go up to the Maritime Centre with me one day? There's a coffee shop that looks out over all this beach and water, and a small museum and gift shop… only if you want to, of course."

It was such a sharp change in the trajectory of the conversation that Naomi needed a moment to let the man's offer settle in and still she was struggling to formulate a suitable response to let him down gently.

"Well, er… Is that Colin?" Naomi peered ahead at a small figure emerging from what looked to be an entrance under the sand dunes. The promenade had veered away by this point, following the steep incline up to the headland.

"Erm, yes, yes, I think it is," Tom looked slightly put out but thankfully said nothing about her lack of response to his invitation.

On closer inspection the hole was a cave, and it was indeed their neighbour hurrying away from the small entrance. He couldn't have looked more furtive if he tried, Naomi thought, with his head down and a small, leather satchel under his arm, sneaking looks behind to see if anyone had spotted his joining the beach.

"Nice evening for it, Colin!" Tom shouted across, with

Naomi having no idea what 'it' was, and doubting her companion did either.

The man in question did a small jump sideways, squinting in their direction until he spotted the pair. He seemed shocked to see them, but soon masked this with a cheery wave and a general comment on the warm weather they were having for the season. Tom angled their trajectory to meet his and Colin plastered a smile on his face. Naomi could tell straight away that it was fake, as the man looked more constipated than happy.

"Yes, lovely evening for a stroll," the keen gardener said, as if trying to convince them that was all he'd been doing.

"It is," Naomi agreed, "and how are you after this morning, Colin?" She was not above poking the beast to get information.

"Well, ah, terrible business that, just terrible, but we march on. I've cooled down now. A lot was said in the heat of the moment… er too much, to be sure. But I intend to smooth it over with Goldie, don't you worry. We'll all be one big, happy family again."

Naomi hadn't been worried, so that was clearly Colin projecting his own fear as they said their goodbyes and continued their walk.

"I don't think we ever were a happy family, or ever will be," Tom said bitterly, before lapsing into silence for the remainder of the stroll.

CHAPTER TWENTY

Naomi was up early the next morning to give Reggie his breakfast and some time out in the back garden. Now that she knew the quick route through the patio door, it was much easier to take the parrot for some free flying. Of course, she had to tell the bird to button his beak, as Goldie's rooms were on the back of the house and Naomi certainly didn't want an early morning encounter with that night owl.

After getting Reggie snuggled back in the bedroom Naomi set out into town, deciding to make the most of market day and grab some fresh fruit and vegetables. First, though, a pit stop in Three B's was necessary to get that strong hit of caffeine to get her through the morning. She was just coming up to the front door of that coffee shop, when who should be leaving but Detective Timpson.

"We'll have to stop meeting like this," Naomi joked, then of course wished she hadn't, as it sounded rather more like flirting than she'd intended.

If he'd noticed, the detective's smile didn't change, as he held the door open for her with his free hand. The other was filled with a large takeaway coffee and a plump paper bag.

"Good morning, Naomi, the team should be up at your place any time now to finish the searching they began yesterday, then I'm heading there myself after conducting a few more interviews so I'll likely see you later."

"Great," Naomi replied, thinking the opposite. The last thing Ginger's needed right now was another shake up to set everyone on edge again.

She pushed that thought from her head, though, as she ducked under Timpson's arm and into the warm refuge of the café. The sky was an overcast grey outside, but inside the many amber fairy lights and the smell of baking bread promised a cosy retreat.

"Naomi," Sarah yawned around the name, "sorry,

excuse me, not much sleep last night."

"Oh? Is everything okay?" Naomi worried.

"Yes, just usual baby feeding and mothering duties, you know."

Naomi didn't know, but she nodded regardless and offered to take the baby for a moment.

"That would be fab, thank you, I need to get some loaves out of the bread oven." Sarah handed little Rose over, who stared at Naomi with big, blue eyes. Copying the movement she had seen Sarah doing when she entered, Naomi rearranged her position until she was holding the infant to her shoulder, and rubbed Rose's back whilst rocking from foot to foot, finding it had the bonus effect of calming herself as well as the baby.

"Aw would you look at that, you're a natural," Sarah beamed at them when she reappeared a few moments later. "Coffee?"

Naomi nodded, careful not to disturb the baby who was drifting off to sleep.

"Sourdough toast with jam? I bet you haven't had any breakfast."

It was true, she hadn't, and Naomi nodded again, grateful for her perceptive new friend.

Other than the noise of the coffee machine and a delicate piano solo coming out of the speakers in the background, the place was a haven of calm and quiet. With Rose now asleep against her, Naomi went to sit on the nearest soft armchair, only to almost fall when her foot tripped on something that filled the whole space under the table and half under the chair too.

"Oh!" She exclaimed in a loud whisper, quickly holding the baby slightly tighter to protect her from the jarring sensation.

"Sorry, that's Dougal, I forgot he was there to be honest. Kath had to go to an appointment."

On closer inspection Naomi saw that the large object was indeed a very curly dog, the same she had seen by the fire in the pub, in fact.

"Bakerslea's own salty sea dog," Naomi continued, "he's a labradoodle. Bit like a big, fluffy toddler really, though he's six now so he's calmed down a bit. He was Jamie's when he lived over at the pub before we were married. Now Kath and I share him."

Sarah didn't look sad at this memory of her late

husband, so Naomi simply smiled and gave her own recollection in return, "My Granny Betty used to have a little terrier called Tina. Bright thing she was, and feisty, so you can imagine how she and Reggie rubbed along – he nicknamed her 'Tina the Terror' and would shriek it whenever he saw her!"

"Oh, that's too funny," Sarah laughed as she took back the baby and snuggled her down in a rocking cradle that was placed just at the end of the counter today, next to their table.

"So, if you're wanting to get to know as many of the locals as possible during your walk around the market, then I'd suggest you start with the local vicar's stall," Naomi began, absentmindedly stroking the huge head of the dog, who had awoken as soon as the scent of hot toast and butter reached his sensitive nose. "It's called Saints and Shells, and he can tell you anything you need to know about the history of the place, in minute detail, as well as showing some fantastic shells he's found on the local beach on his many prayer walks."

"Really?" Naomi didn't sound convinced.

"No, I'm having fun with you," Sarah giggled, and apologised, "Father Daniels is lovely, but if you stop there you'll get nothing else done. He could talk the hind leg off a donkey. He's very passionate about local history."

"Well, that might come in handy one day, but today is definitely not that day," Naomi lifted her plate just in time before her last piece of toast was surreptitiously swept away by an undercover labradoodle.

"Dougal! Be polite!" Sarah scolded the giant dog gently, earning herself not a small amount of side eye as the dog huffed off to lie alongside the counter, stretching out to the full length of that bench.

"So, I heard about the poison being found up at your place, word travels fast in these small towns," Sarah whispered as she sipped her vanilla latte.

"Doesn't it just," Naomi agreed. "Yes it was all rather... well, nasty, to be honest. A lot of blame flying around, and not enough thinking about the discovery as actual evidence. Detective Timpson wasn't best pleased. And of course, it points a fresh finger to the manor as housing the murderer."

"Which I imagine isn't so great when you live there," Sarah said.

"Exactly, hence why I'm about to wander round the market for a couple of hours. If I feel like staying out longer, I may even have a chat with this Father Daniels you mentioned!" They both laughed, waking Rose who started to fuss and squirm.

"Thank you for the chat," Naomi said, finishing the last dregs of her mocha.

"Anytime, Naomi, we're always here."

CHAPTER TWENTY-ONE

Naomi returned back to the manor house just as Detective Timpson's car was pulling up outside, her good mood evaporating at the sight. With her hands full of bags of fresh produce, and her hair plastered to her face from the unexpected downpour on her walk back, for the second time that day Naomi thanked the man for opening a door for her. Inside Ginger's all was quiet, save for the faint sound of an upbeat tune coming from the ballroom. Timpson helped her deposit her bags in the kitchen, then asked Naomi to round up everyone who was in the house and bring them to the ballroom.

Naomi felt the familiar ball of dread grow in her stomach, even knowing she herself had done nothing wrong.

"This place is not good for my anxiety," she had not meant to say the statement out loud, and received a sympathetic look from the detective, who passed her at the bottom of the stairs presumably on his way to the conservatory or to Colin's office.

Carys offered to go and wake Goldie, for which Naomi was especially grateful. That left just Tom on their floor, and Reggie to check on. Knocking on her neighbour's bedroom door and getting no answer, Naomi was about to hurry to her own room, when a sleepy voice said, "Come in."

"Oh, sorry to wake you," Naomi said, popping her head round the door and getting the full view of Tom stretching in bed, bare from the waist up. "The police are here, need us in the ballroom," this she spoke through the wood of the door, her view safely on the corridor side again.

"Sorry, day off, lie in. No worries, give me five."

Naomi tried to scrub the image of his tousled bed hair and muscular chest from her mind, wondering when the man found time to work out. *Presumably at the police gym,* she thought, though why it interested her she couldn't say.

With Reggie pacified with an early lunch, excited to see the fresh blueberries Naomi had brought, her own feet were heavy as she descended the stairs and headed to the ballroom.

"One-two-cha-cha-cha, four beats, five steps, my darling… No, right foot first, my left, your right…" Alfonso appeared to be ignoring the assembling group as he continued to focus on his current dance student, an elderly woman who looked thoroughly confused.

"I think that's enough of that," Timpson said, striding into the room and fixing his gaze on Alfonso. "I'm surprised you have time for dance lessons, as you didn't manage to fit in a visit to the station to see me yesterday. I'm even more shocked that you seem to think it's business as usual. Thank you, Mrs. Gibbings, I think it best if my officer takes you back to the retirement home now."

"Well, I really!" The Italian blustered, "I gotten no such message to make trip to police office."

Timpson gave him a look of disdaining disbelief, before turning to the rest of them and asking everyone to sit at one of the round afternoon tea tables. Naomi noticed as she moved to sit down that three uniformed officers now stood by the door, blocking anyone who may wish to exit the ballroom, and it did nothing to calm her anxiety.

Tom sat next to her, in joggers and a t-shirt, his hair still not having seen a comb, whilst Carys was on Naomi's other side, her gaze fixed dead ahead and telltale tear tracks down her cheeks. Next to her, Goldie fussed with her bouncy blow-dry. Their boss wore a lurid purple and pink striped robe, though her face was made up and she had returned to wearing her distinctive, gaudy jewellery. Today's earrings reached almost to the woman's jawline, a waterfall of amethysts and rubies descending from each ear. Beside her, Alfonso bounced up and down in his seat as if he had ants in his pants, whilst between him and Tom, Colin looked stoney-faced, several twigs stuck in his olive green jumper.

Since the tables only sat six, Detective Timpson pulled up a chair from a nearby table and everyone shuffled to make a space for him between Tom and Colin.

"Well, isn't this cosy," Goldie said, "if I'd known we were getting together I'd have had Carys prepare a brunch."

Naomi shot the woman a look which said 'really?' just

as the far door to the room opened and the police officers moved to let a breathless Argyll in to join them all.

"Apologies, Sir, forensics have only just finished with it," the detective said, handing Timpson a paper bag and then almost collapsing onto the nearest chair at the next table.

"Right, perfect time actually Argyll," Timpson declared, "now we can begin."

With all eyes on him, the detective took a deep breath and launched into his grand reveal, in the style of the great literary detectives of decades gone by.

"So, I wanted you all here to hear this, so that the nasty mess is cleared up once and for all. No more pointing fingers. You will all find out together and can hopefully draw a line under the grisly incident and begin afresh. I appreciate, for some, the past few days have weighed heavily on their hearts and have adversely affected their mental health, which is very understandable." He didn't turn to look at Naomi, yet she had the distinct impression Timpson was referencing her. She felt her face flush red and clasped her hands in her lap tightly.

"So," the detective continued, "a pot of rat poison, still

three quarters full, was found here in the conservatory yesterday. The conservation of the item as evidence was in no way preserved, nevertheless, we found our Means, our weapon so to speak and the location pointed to someone with free access to that room, someone likely sitting at this table now. So, let us move on to the Method of administering the poison," Timpson lifted the paper bag, and produced from inside a clear plastic box. Nestling within that was a shiny, flat object which looked exactly like the mysterious item on Tom's photograph, from the little Naomi had been able to see, at least.

"Located under the driver's seat of the limousine in which the deceased woman was travelling, on the floor of the passenger footwell, was this make-up compact. Testing has shown the face powder inside to have been mixed with sufficient quantity of rat poison that, if applied regularly, would have the cumulative effect of causing death."

Only Naomi and Carys gasped at that new information. Goldie was picking at her pointed, acrylic nails, whilst the men remained stoic.

"So, we can assume from her husband's statement, that the deceased had been using this for the few days before her death as that was when her headaches, confusion and nosebleeds had started suddenly. With the poison carefully mixed with the makeup, and then covered with a layer of the real powder only, we can assume that the deceased applied it to her face either just before being collected that lunchtime, or in her first couple of minutes in the car. By this day, she must have reached the fully poisonous layer, and so death quickly followed, building on the toxicity already in her system. All following?"

There was a general nod of heads, as Carys whispered, "This is so awful," and Naomi gave the housekeeper's hand a squeeze.

"Very good, now we have the Means. So, the victim's husband swears to never having seen the antique powder compact before. It's quite distinctive, too, can you see? Gold edging with enamelled teal hummingbirds inlaid. Something very memorable, I would imagine. This means the deceased had never used the item in front of her husband, had never mentioned buying it, leading us to believe she had reason to keep it secret, wouldn't you agree? Now, why would a married woman keep a gift a secret, I wonder? And, more importantly, who could have gifted it to her?" He paused there, for dramatic effect no doubt, and scanned everyone at the table.

Colin remained unmoved, his face unreadable, whilst Alfonso had drips of sweat trailing down his forehead and leaving tracks in the man's orange self-tan – or stage make-up, Naomi wasn't sure which – to reveal his own pale skin beneath.

"Should I make us all some tea?" Carys whispered.

"Not quite yet, Mrs. Evans, just bear with me a few moments longer," Timpson asked kindly.

"Could I, ah, be excused for a moment?" Goldie asked, pushing her chair back abruptly. The woman's hands shaking as she stood. Her usual emotional support cat had not been seen in the public rooms since having been recovered from the conservatory yesterday, and Naomi was glad of it. An angrier animal she had never come across – not even Reggie when he was told his fruit source had dried up.

"If accompanied by an officer, then yes," Timpson agreed. Naomi caught the brief flash of excitement on the man's face before he hid it once again behind his professional façade. "Now, I wonder what Mrs. Hornsley could have remembered so suddenly?" The detective let the rhetorical question hang in the thick air.

CHAPTER TWENTY-TWO

It felt like hours when in fact it was probably only a few minutes before Goldie returned to her seat. In front of her on the table she gently placed a flat, round, shiny object.

"Well, well, well," Timpson said, "I wonder what this could be?" He gestured to Argyll who hurried to collect the item and pass it to him.

Timpson made a show of examining the object, before describing it slowly, "Gold trim, enamel birds, pink this time, make-up compact. It looks like someone got a job lot at the antiques store, assuming they aren't just cheap, modern replicas of course. I hope you've not been using this, Mrs. Hornsley?"

Goldie shook her head, no, then added, "I put it straight in a drawer when I received it, I don't like using old make-up, full of bacteria."

"A wise move," the detective confirmed, then passed the compact to Argyll who produced a clear plastic evidence bag from the inside pocket of her voluminous coat and deposited the item inside. "That will be tested for poison, too, though I have a feeling this one will be purely make-up. I'm pretty certain the killer didn't want you dead, Mrs. Hornsley, likely only wished to bribe you with a pretty trinket to convince you to let him have free lodging in this old house. No, only the woman who had found out his thieving ways was to be eliminated in his dastardly plan. So, please do share with the group... Who gave you the compact?"

Goldie looked wildly around the circle, clearly hoping someone would save her from having to be the one to expose the murderer. Everyone avoided eye contact with the woman, though, until at last, exasperated, Timpson snapped at her, "Now! Please, Mrs. Hornsley!"

"I, um, well," Goldie looked pleadingly at Timpson, then at Colin, and finally at Alfonso, where her gaze remained. "It was Mr. Di Marco, my dance tutor."

"What?" The Italian shrieked, standing quickly so that his chair fell backwards, "No, no, no, these are the lies! I have never before seen one of these littles, how you call them, compacts! Never before! I may borrow some sparkly items from my ladies once in a while to help with the renting, but only when absolutely necessary! No deaths needed!"

"That's enough, save it for the station. Arrest him, please, Argyll," Timpson ignored the man's loud protestations as the other detective, aided by two uniformed officers, read the Italian his rights and took him away.

Undeterred, Timpson continued his monologue from earlier, "So, now we have the third 'M', Motive. Mr. Di Marco there is as light-fingered as he is light-footed. Being behind on his rent at the caravan site, and owing Mrs. Hornsley here for use of the ballroom for his lessons, the money from his dancing students was simply not enough. Lucky for him, then, that he worked in such close proximity with these fawning ladies that it was easy to slip off a bracelet here, a ring there. Had you noticed anything missing, Mrs. Hornsley?"

"No, no, I hadn't," Goldie shook her head, her eyes

wide with shock.

"Well, I would venture to claim that the late Mrs. Bonham-Smythe had, and that she threatened to use that knowledge to expose Mr. Di Marco. Knowing that that would be the final nail in the coffin of his time here, so to speak, the desperate man gave her the compact ostensibly as a way to make amends. To apologise and beg that she not expose him as a thief to both her husband and to Di Marco's other clients. Obviously his real reasoning behind the gift was a lot more sinister.

"Oh my goodness!" Carys clasped her hand to her chest. "I'm glad now that I couldn't afford his lessons!"

It was almost too much to take in, Naomi agreed, though it did all make sense.

"Well, that's that then," Colin stood, "I assume we are free to leave now? Hopefully this draws the final curtain on the whole pantomime."

"Indeed," Timpson nodded, "and I thank you all for your cooperation." He turned and walked away then, following the remaining police officer out of the ballroom and leaving them all in a state of stunned silence.

"That was, um, rather intense for a Saturday morning," Tom said as he climbed the main staircase behind Naomi.

"It really was," Naomi agreed.

"And I mean, why couldn't he have offed Goldie at the same time? The man had the plan, he could've killed two birds with one stone," Tom whispered.

Shocked, Naomi paused on the top step and looked back at him, knowing her expression was incredulous.

"I just mean, I'm sure she's just as deserving as that other woman," Tom tried to backtrack, but instead ended up digging the hole deeper for himself.

Naomi said nothing, simply turning her back to him and hurrying to her own bedroom, keen to feel the reassurance of Reggie's squishy soft face against her cheek.

"Bad bird!" The parrot squawked upon seeing her, though he flew straight to Naomi's shoulder and snuggled into the crook of her neck.

"I know, I'm sorry I left you. What a mess, eh Reggie? Maybe we should go home to Baker's Rise after all? Back to Flora and Adam."

"My Flora, love you!"

"I know, I love mum too, but do I want to admit defeat right now? Should I wait and see how things pan out?"

"My No Me! My Flora! So cosy!" The little parrot chirped, and Naomi wished – and not for the first time either – that her world view could be as simple as his bird's-eye one.

CHAPTER TWENTY-THREE

"About yesterday," Tom began, but Naomi blanked him as they entered the ballroom the next afternoon, summoned by Colin and Goldie to a crisis meeting.

Naomi had stayed in her room the whole of the previous evening, grateful to Carys who brought her a tray of food, whilst she procrastinated her decision.

"Right, I'll get straight to it," Colin said once they were all assembled, in a rather unsettling déjà-vu of the previous day, though thankfully minus a police presence. "In case anyone is thinking of skedaddling, then you can think again because Goldie and I have agreed to give the place another go. No grand openings or the like, we'll just launch into the original plan for the venue as soon as Goldie can source another couple of dance tutors. In the meantime, we'll be giving each of you a proper budget moving forward, plus a clear schedule of what is required and when. There will be new contracts for you, Naomi and Carys, and Tom you will be given proper notice of when your photography skills will be required at afternoon teas and the occasional evening dance. I trust that is all in order?" He looked at them all sternly, like a headmaster addressing unruly pupils, and almost daring anyone to object.

Goldie had remained uncharacteristically silent, stroking Ginger who was asleep on her lap. For once, the woman was dressed in daytime clothes and her jewellery was so subtle she could almost have fitted in with a normal office environment. The cat, it appeared, now had an electronic location tracking tag attached to her diamante collar, like a prisoner on parole. Naomi felt sympathetic towards the fluffy felon, who really hadn't done anything other than make a bid for freedom.

Colin's plans all sounded fine, but Naomi wasn't so easily won over as the other two, who each had their own reasons for staying and were nodding in compliance, albeit decidedly half-heartedly.

"And why should we believe anything will change?" Naomi addressed her question to the organ grinder and not the monkey.

Goldie slowly raised her gaze to meet hers and tipped her head to the side to study Naomi carefully, "Well, my dear, it is your choice whether you stay or not. Whether you want to be here or not. Whether you believe this venue can work, or not."

"Ah, but we value your skills as a baker..." Colin attempted to pour oil on troubled waters.

"Patisserie chef," Naomi interrupted him.

"Yes, indeed, and as such you will receive the ingredients you require and a salary commensurate with your experience."

"Have you suddenly found a pot of gold?" Tom asked sarcastically.

Colin gave him a harsh glare and ignored the question, continuing to direct his reassurances at Naomi, "Really, I can assure you..."

"Your assurances mean little to me, I'll need to see the new systems in action. You have me now on a trial basis of two months," Naomi felt the nerves fluttering inside her and hoped they didn't show on her face or in her voice, "and by that I mean, you have to stick to your word for everyone. I'm not prepared to watch Carys being taken for granted any longer."

"Oh, I'm fine…" the Welshwoman began.

"No, Naomi is right," Colin butted in, "our fresh start will be for everyone."

And so it was that Naomi found herself committed to sticking around at Ginger's, which was what she had half decided to do anyway. When her parents made their weekly phone call she had decided she would offer to keep Reggie for another month or so, explaining that he was good for her wellbeing, though omitting the bit about having been in the centre of a murder investigation. No need to worry them with that. She would play down her concerns and stress the positives of her new position, like her friendship with Sarah, and would promise to come home for Christmas. It was just a few short months till then anyway.

Unbeknownst to her, though, fate had other plans…
There was still plenty of time left in the year for another murder.

EPILOGUE

It was a chilly October day a few weeks later, the type of weather where the rain hits sideways and the leaves are a slippery mush on the pavement, that Naomi found herself sitting on a table next to Detective Timpson in the Three B's café. Bouncing little Rose on her lap as Sarah packed the loaf orders, Naomi marvelled at how fast the baby was growing.

"She's sleeping a bit better too, now that I've introduced solids," Sarah explained, waving at her daughter from behind the counter.

Timpson, who had so far been drinking his coffee in silence, spoke up then, "She's the image of you, has your beautiful eyes," before going back to reading his newspaper.

Sarah's cheeks blushed pink as she and Naomi shared a wide-eyed look, one that said they were going to be discussing that remark once the man had left. Naomi presumed Timpson didn't know Sarah's history and that she was a widow whose heart likely still remained with her late husband.

"Are you a regular here now, Detective?" Naomi asked, to fill the now awkward silence.

"Well, the coffee's great, as is the service," the man smiled up at Sarah, though she was pretending to busy herself with the bread orders, "plus my wife used to love this beach, we used to come here a lot when we were courting. I'd deliberately avoided it for the past year or so for that very reason, but having been brought back for the murder case, it's become one of my favourite haunts again. I'm trying to focus on the good memories."

It was the most personal thing the detective had ever shared with either of them, and Sarah spun around immediately to face the man.

"You lost your wife?" She whispered.

"I did, to cancer," he replied softly, holding Sarah's

gaze for longer than usual.

Perhaps he does know about Jamie, Naomi mused silently, watching the unspoken exchange between the pair.

"So, you decided to stay," Timpson suddenly changed the subject, and Naomi took a moment to realise he was addressing his question to her.

"Oh me? Yes, just on a trial basis. My only other option is back to Baker's Rise, so I decided I might as well give Ginger's another go now that the business is being taken seriously. How is the case going? All done and dusted?"

"Well, we charged the man. No confession but CPS said it's not required given the evidence. A few of the man's other dance students – all in their seventies or eighties, I might add, and not all of them in full control of their faculties – realised they were missing jewellery when they checked. And he admits the deceased called him out on it. So, case closed as far as my team are concerned. An investigation so neat and tidy you could tie it up with a bow."

"But isn't there such a thing as too neat? Too tidy?" Naomi wondered aloud. "Like everything just fell into place too perfectly? I mean, what about the man's vehement denials?"

"Fake, like the rest of him. Turns out he was born in Essex, to Italian parents but even so… I don't care that he trained in Milan, he's still a murderer," Timpson said emphatically. "When you have Motive, Means and Method, it's clear-cut."

"The man did seem… a bit too dramatic to be real, almost like a caricature of himself," Naomi agreed, "but then, so does Goldie. Well, she did until she got her act together."

"Oh? Still opening the venue as a dance hall?" Timpson asked.

"Yep, next week, let's hope it's smooth sailing," Naomi raised an eyebrow, insinuating she had her doubts on that front.

"Indeed," Timpson agreed, "we wouldn't want it failing on the second attempt, would we?"

*If you'd like to find out whether Ginger's is a go-go and if Naomi and Reggie are destined for a simple life in Bakerslea-By-The Sea, join them in the next Baker's SurpRISE book, "**Afternoon Absentea**," available from Spring 2025.*

Have you visited Baker's Rise, where it all began?

*Read on for an excerpt of "**Here Today, Scone Tomorrow**," and see how Reggie came flying into Flora's life!*

R. A. Hutchins

AN EXCERPT FROM *HERE TODAY, SCONE TOMORROW*

Stan Houghton stormed out of the front door of the manor house known as 'The Rise' and strode off down the gravel driveway. His face, a molten red from his latest showdown with the 'lord of the manor' Harold Baker, contorted into a furious visage which matched his balled fists and heavy breathing. Surprised to see a familiar figure, dressed to the nines, approaching from the other direction, Stan tried to rein in his temper whilst making pleasantries.

"Good morning, Mrs. Edwards, fine day," he did not pause even for a second as they passed each other, nor did Stan listen for a reply as he hurried off back to the farm.

"If that's you again Houghton, you can get lost!" the shouted warning from indoors could be heard behind the flaking wooden main door of the manor, as its next visitor waited patiently on the doorstep.

"Oh, hello," his greeting was hardly welcoming even when Harold did pull the door open, "you'd better come in then!" He stalked into the main drawing room, eyeing his pet parrot suspiciously as if an outburst might ensue, and muttering, "not a word," as Harold waggled his finger in the direction of his feathered friend's perch.

The parrot, taking only one fleeting look at the outstretched finger, and choosing to also ignore the hastily given warning completely, screeched, "Old trout! Old trout!" and rose from his perch, flapping his wings viciously around the head of the woman who had just entered the room.

"Enough!" Harold said sternly, and the parrot finally decided to cease his assault.

"I gather this isn't a great time? I suppose Farmer Houghton was commenting on your latest rent increases for the village?" The woman tried surreptitiously to restore the elaborate up-do which the stupid parrot had managed to make look like a bird's nest. Giving up, she continued, "With the number of fields he has, I'd wager he's sorely affected." She stated it as a matter of fact, apparently unmoved by either the rent situation or the plight of a neighbour.

"Aye, well, he's always here threatening when the prices go up, but he pays it in the end. Just like they all do, if they want to keep living in Baker's Rise."

"Quite so. Anyhow, I've been baking and thought you might like a scone or two?"

Harold tried to hide his surprise. It was not a common occurrence for villagers to make their way up the hill for anything other than to air their gripes, let alone such a comely example of womanhood. For a moment, Harold was lost in sweet reminiscence of his many dalliances in years gone by. He was old now, stout in the waist and grizzly of feature, so he very much doubted that was what was on offer here. Nevertheless, he was intrigued as to what exactly would warrant such a special visit.

"Thank you kindly, dear lady, please take a seat and I will prepare a pot of tea," Harold licked his lips as he took in the sight of her, her face all made up to show her features at their best, her body encased in a tight tweed suit. When the lady didn't immediately sit, he was confused for a moment, until he realised that she would need to perch on top of one of the many mounds of paperwork, old magazines and newspapers which littered every available surface. Quickly, Harold swept a pile of brochures from the end of a settee and rushed off to the kitchen.

When he returned, the scones were arranged on one of the fine china plates, inherited from his mother, and which were stored in glass-fronted cabinets all around the room. Jam and butter – which she must have brought with her – sat in two dainty dishes complete with a miniature silver spoon and knife. *Aye, she's after something,* Harold thought to himself, his mind whirring with what he might get in return, as he set the tray on the small walnut coffee table between them, also cleared of its mound of papers hastily, and took his usual seat on a sagging Chesterfield.

"Shall I be mother?" she said coyly, fluttering her eyelashes at him.

Harold almost blushed like a schoolboy, "Indeed, madam, thank you kindly."

As she poured the tea and added the five sugar cubes which he requested, Harold thought he detected a small tremor in the lady's hands. Assuming it was a nervous anticipation for what was surely about to pass between them, Harold bestowed upon her his most gracious smile, which some rather ungrateful females had in the past told him more resembled a leer. Accepting the cup and saucer gratefully, and the proffered scone, Harold settled back into his chair.

"So, my dear, what brings you up here?"

Instead of answering, the woman simply looked on as

Harold's hand reached to his mouth and he took a huge bite of the baked treat.

"You do," she whispered, as Harold felt his breath begin to shorten, his chest to tighten, his tongue to swell and his throat to close.

The dropped plate smashed on the parquet floor, as Harold grasped his throat and managed to gargle, "What the..?" He staggered towards his guest, who simply moved out of his range.

"Peanut," she spoke clearly and with a sadistic smile, as Harold noticed for the first time the smudge of bright red lipstick on the woman's teeth, as if it had been applied by someone unused to doing so. It made her look like one of those clowns in a horror film. Why he would notice that, of all things now, Harold wondered as he collapsed to the floor, his body convulsing.

The last things he saw were her stilettoed feet stepping over him as the woman went to retrieve the rest of the scones, and the china cups and saucers for washing. She reached down to check Harold's pulse, giving a nod of approval as she found none, before quickly collecting up the fallen remnants along with the broken pieces of crockery, and leaving the room silently.

Nought could be heard but the ticking of the antique Grandfather clock in the corner and the squawk of the parrot, shouting "Peanut" on repeat.

Ten Months Later

Flora looked around her at the six small tables, all set out with fine china cups and saucers in co-ordinating colours, lace doilies, floral tablecloths and silver cutlery. She smiled to herself, content in all she had achieved since coming to Baker's Rise a few months ago. The tearoom in the old stables, closed up for several years, had been given a new lease of life with a fresh lick of paint and bunting hung around the rough walls. A new sign had been hung outside the door, advertising the 'Tearoom on The Rise' – Flora liked to keep things simple and elegant. She ran her hands down her smart apron and patted her hair to ensure she was as smart as possible, before checking her watch for the fifth time in as many minutes. Still half an hour remained till opening time. The local baker, George Jones, had dropped off the day's delicacies an hour ago, and Flora had already arranged them in the display cabinet and fridge. Scones with clotted cream from the local farm and jam from the farm shop, teacakes, iced buns, custard tarts... a whole list of tempting treats for what Flora hoped would be her many customers, keen to try out the new tearoom on opening day. Flora wished to be baking some of the goods herself before too long, once she'd found someone in the village to teach her. She would start out as easily as possible, she had decided, and try to perfect the traditional English scone.

Flora had advertised the tearoom's opening in the local parish newsletter, the aptly titled, "What's on the Rise in Baker's Rise," as well as on the church notice board. She had tried to spread the news by word of mouth too, though this was more difficult as Flora was new to the village. She had quickly realised that folk here were not too keen on newcomers. Trust had to be earned, and civility only turned to friendship when you had embedded yourself suitably in village life. Flora hoped desperately that this would be a quicker process for her than for most, since she wished the tearoom to become a hub of village life. Mindful that any customers would have to travel halfway up the small hill, The Rise, to reach her, she had already thought about special offers and loyalty schemes to tempt people her way. Probably getting ahead of herself, Flora knew, but after coming from a fast-paced and highly structured job in the city, she was already struggling to fill her days and occupy her quick mind.

The bell on the door chimed and Flora was shocked from her musings. It was still too early for customers.

"Flora? Are you here?" The polished tone of the local solicitor, Harry Bentley, put Flora at her ease as she rushed from behind the counter to greet him. His grey hair popped around the door which he had only opened a fraction, followed by his wide-rimmed spectacles and his red, bulbous nose.

"Harry! What a lovely surprise!" the elderly gent, who should have been long since retired by now but still took an interest in the affairs of the village residents, had been Flora's sole friend and confidant since she'd arrived. It was he who had originally contacted her about the estate, he who had advised she should keep her true identity a secret until she had been accepted by the villagers. Harry had arranged the refurbishment of the coach house for Flora per her instructions from London, and had suggested the tearoom as a viable business opportunity. He had met her when she arrived and had visited her several times since, always with a friendly smile and a word of advice.

"Just thought I'd come to wish you luck on your first day, dear! Well, doesn't it look splendid! Very pretty indeed."

"Oh thank you, Harry, it wouldn't be anything without your recommendations and advice. Thank you for suggesting the farm shop, by the way, the jam and honey is delicious!"

"Not at all, my dear, now where are we with all the paperwork up at the big house?"

"Well, as you know there is mounds of it, I have only been able to shift the tip of the iceberg really. I know, it's my own fault. Being an actuary for so many years, I can't throw a single sheet of paper away without first reading what's on it! It makes the process slow and laborious, but I'm not in a hurry. The whole place is becoming dilapidated anyway. As you know, I've used the funds I could get my hands on to do up the coach house and this stable block. I'll have to wait to receive my divorce settlement before I can begin anything else. Hopefully, the villagers will have accepted me by then and it won't need to be so cloak and dagger," she gave a rueful smile and offered Harry a coffee from the new machine, which Flora had only just begun to learn how to use.

Eyeing the large silver monstrosity with distrust, Harry opted for a cup of tea, and sat down at the table nearest the counter.

"Aye, you've accomplished a lot in a few months, slow and steady wins the race especially in a place like Baker's Rise!"

"Indeed," Flora joined him at the table, a pot of tea for two and two toasted teacakes set in front of them. They chatted happily, until Flora looked at her watch and realised she should have changed the small sign on the door to 'open' some fifteen minutes ago. Not that she need worry, it was hardly as if she had a queue of customers waiting outside.

"I'll go and leave you to it. Remember to phone me if you need anything. On my home phone, mind, I still haven't worked out this mobile thing that my nephew gave me."

"Thank you, Harry," Flora busied herself clearing the table as she heard Harry's old BMW driving away on the gravel driveway. She took a deep breath, closed her eyes, and prayed that luck would be on her side and bring her some customers on her first day…

ABOUT THE AUTHOR

Rachel Hutchins lives in northeast England with her husband, three children and their dog Boudicca. She loves writing both mysteries and romances, and enjoys reading these genres too! Her favourite place is walking along the local coastline, with a coffee and some cake!

You can connect with via her website at: www.authorrachelhutchins.com

Alternatively, she has social media pages on:

Facebook: www.facebook.com/rahutchinsauthor

Instagram: www.instagram.com/ra_hutchins_author

OTHER MURDER MYSTERIES BY R.A. HUTCHINS

Fresh As A Daisy – The Lillymouth Mysteries Trilogy Book One

When Reverend Daisy Bloom arrives at her new parish of Lillymouth to see that a recently deceased body has been discovered in the graveyard, she finds herself needing to do some sleuthing amidst her sermons.

Reacquainting herself with the painful memories of her childhood home whilst trying to make a fresh start, Daisy leans on old friends and new companions. Playing the part of amateur sleuth was never in her plan, but needs must if she is to ever focus on her own agenda.

Will her new vocation be able to protect Daisy from the spirits of the past, or was her return to her home town on the Yorkshire coast always destined for disaster?

Furthermore, are her new neighbours all as they seem, or are they harbouring secrets which may be their own undoing? Worse still, will they also lead to Daisy's demise?

A tale of homecoming and homicide, of suspense and secrets, this is the first book in the Lillymouth

Mysteries Series.

Note from the Author: Since the same cast of characters feature in each book of this series, and there are some overarching mysteries threaded throughout the books, the stories are best read in

No Shrinking Violet – The Lillymouth Mysteries Trilogy Book Two

With a new, unexpected ally, a housekeeper who enjoys amateur sleuthing and the unwanted affections of an otherwise aloof vicarage cat, Reverend Daisy Bloom is back in this second book of the popular Lillymouth Mysteries series.

Tensions are high in Lillymouth as some of the locals attempt to move a group of environmental activists who have settled on the headland just outside of town. Leading the way is Violet Glendinning, wife of the local bank manager, head of the parish council, and self-appointed protector of 'the way things used to be.'

Daisy is reluctantly given the role of keeper of the peace, though she would much rather be focusing on her own personal conflicts.

When one of the newcomers is found dead shortly after an altercation with Violet, it is not long before she finds herself faced with uncomfortable enquiries.

Will Violet swallow her pride and ask Reverend Daisy for help, or will it prove too bitter a pill to swallow?

Chin Up Buttercup – The Lillymouth Mysteries Trilogy Book Three

The shocking finale of the Lillymouth Mysteries trilogy is here, and Reverend Daisy will need all the support she can get if she is to escape unscathed.

A late night arrival leads a reluctant Daisy to the crime scene of another murder. Unfortunately for the vicar, she recognises the body as a longtime foe and kneeling beside the deceased is definitely the last place she should be found.

Quickly realising she has been set up, Daisy must uncover the identity of her backstabbing adversary before it's too late. Has she been altogether too trusting of those around her? Has she underestimated her haters in the parish? Or is the answer to another secret about to be revealed?

Not knowing who to trust, Daisy shuns all help, deciding to go it alone this time. Will this prove to be a costly mistake or a wise choice? Only time will tell.

And the clock is ticking.

Printed in Great Britain
by Amazon